OTHER CHILDREN'S FICTION BY ANDREW SALKEY

Hurricane, 1964
Earthquake, 1965
Drought, 1966
The Shark Hunters, 1966
Jonah Simpson, 1970
Joey Tyson, 1974
The River That Disappeared, 1979
Danny Jones, 1980

ANDREW SALKEY

RIOT

ILLUSTRATED BY WILLIAM PAPAS

PEEPAL TREE

First published in Great Britain in 1967
by Oxford University Press
This new edition published in 2011
Peepal Tree Press Ltd
17 King's Avenue
Leeds LS6 1QS
England

ISBN13: 9781845231811

Supported by
**ARTS COUNCIL
ENGLAND**

CONTENTS

To Eliot and Jason

Difficulties and dangers are the hazards (of the new spirit of the people) – more life its aim.

It takes a mighty fire
To create a great people.

PROLOGUE

1

For a long time, life had been extremely miserable for the vast majority of the working people in Kingston and for the peasantry in the rural parishes.

Gerald's father, Martin Manson, had told him one morning after breakfast, 'All this exploitation and poverty just can't go on much longer, Gerry. There's bound to be a right royal upheaval sooner or later, and it's going to come from the Union.'

In spite of the fact that the Union had not yet been formed,

Gerald's father thought, planned and acted as if he were an active Union member, and he also professed his great confidence in the foresight and integrity of the leader, Alexander Crossman.

2

Alexander Crossman and Martin Manson had been old shipmates on the Banana Boat line which ran its cargo-and-passenger service between Jamaica and the United Kingdom. Crossman had left his job as a cargo-hand on the *Jamaica Commerce* and had become a reputable cabinet-maker and the founder-leader of the Crossman Industrial Trades Union; Martin Manson had also left the *Commerce* and had become the chief works'-engineer at the Kingston Foundry and the shop steward for the C.I.T.U. there.

3

Gerald's mother, Jessica Manson, was a teacher of general subjects in a Kingston west end boys' school.

Gerald was in the Fourth Form at Kingston College. His two best friends, who were not only his form-mates but also his neighbours on either side of his house, were Arnold Palmer, who was better known as 'Shifty Shanks' the fastest hundred yards' sprinter in the Fourth Year, and Leo Lockwood who was called 'Fu Manchu' because of the inscrutable expression he always wore during the Maths and English Grammar periods.

Shifty and Fu were Gerald's constant companions, but Gerald was also rather close to his father and to his hectic world of local politics and work problems. Gerald often talked to him about the various topics concerning Union rules and industrial relations, and always his father would end by saying, 'There's bound to be a right royal upheaval sooner or later, and it's going to come from the Union.'

Those were the words which were echoing in Gerald's head, late on the last Friday afternoon in May, as he rode his scholarship Rudge Whitworth through the front gate of his college on his way home to Cross Roads.

PART ONE

THE MAN IN WHITE

CHAPTER ONE

1

Sitting well back from the sparkling chromium handle of the bicycle, with his hands resting stylishly akimbo, Gerald cruised left along North Street, turned right, into Orange Street, and headed towards Slipe Road.

Ordinarily he would have been riding home with Shifty Shanks and Fu Manchu, and together they would be belting along like circus riders and challenging passing buses and cars and other cyclists to short sprints between stop-signs, but Gerald was on his

own because Shifty had been asked by the sports' master to remain behind for a late workout on the 'hundred' and 'two-twenty' training tracks, and because Fu had been detained by the English master for an extra grammar lesson.

Even though Gerald was relaxed, he was also deeply thoughtful all along the way; he was thinking about his father's words and trying to imagine what the upheaval would look like when it came; he was tilting his head a little arrogantly, and he never once held the black rubber handle-grips. It was fashionable for the more confident cyclists to be seen cruising effortlessly with perfect balance and with a hint of devil-may-care, and Gerald was no exception. He continued his 'no hands' ride even while he was going up the rise on Slipe Road, which detracted very slightly from his poise, though he had to pedal with extra force. This he did with concealed effort, still appearing to be cruising along coolly. Just as he was passing the front gate of Saint Luke's Church, an old beggar waved his stick and shouted, 'Young boy, you t'ink you' in a circus or wha'? Mind show-off don't kill you!' Gerald smiled and waved. The old man frowned and turned to watch Gerald's daring progress up the road. As he got nearer to the criss-crossing of the traffic at Cross Roads, Gerald merely placed the tip of the forefinger of his right hand on the ring-ridge in the middle of the handle, to ensure at least minimum control of the bicycle, and kept going at the same speed; the old man noticed Gerald's compromise and he chuckled and nodded to himself as he walked into the churchyard. Gerald negotiated the cross currents at the centre of the swirl of the traffic and then he took his fingertip off the ring-ridge of the handle and cruised the last three hundred yards, over Cross Roads, to the side gate of his house on Half Way Tree Road.

He hopped backwards off the saddle, while the bicycle was still in motion, curling his fingers lightly around the slender stem of the saddle-post and running behind the back wheel. He always dismounted while the bicycle was in motion; all the riders who rode with style dismounted like that.

Shifty Shanks and Fu Manchu both rode Rudge Whitworths. But Gerald's Rudge was his 'iron horse'; he knew it intimately; he knew every shudder the ratchet, sprocket and chain gave, every seemingly unaccountable swerve of the front wheel, every listing movement of the frame. He was sensitive to an under-inflated tyre, and even to a loose spoke in either of the rims.

After he had won a scholarship to Kingston College, his father had given him the Rudge and had made him promise to take good care of it throughout his school career. 'Ride it the way you use your scholarship,' his father had told him, 'and I'll know exactly how you're doing at school without having to ask you a word.' They had both laughed self-consciously at the time. Later on, however, when Gerald had thought about his father's advice, he wondered seriously just what possible link there could be between his schoolwork and the way in which he would take care

of his bicycle, but he gave up puzzling over the matter after he had convinced himself, reassuringly dishonestly, that his father had *only* been trying to caution him indirectly about the urgency of riding safely on the roads.

He leant his bicycle against the side of the house and untied the bundle of his text- and exercise-books which hung neatly from an old Sea Scouts' leather belt, coiled round the crossbar

13

of the frame. He clasped the books under his arm, patted the saddle and walked round to the back of the house.

2

'Supper firs', clean down the Rudge nex', an' homework las'?' Miriam, the cook, asked him, as he bounded up the steps of the back veranda. 'Or homework firs', then the Rudge, an' supper las'?'

'The Rudge first, Miriam,' he said, winking and hoping to soften her up. 'Homework, and supper when the Old Lady and the Old Man come in.'

'By that, I take it you mean you' *mother* an' you' *father*?' Miriam asked bluntly.

'Yes. I mean Mama and Dad.'

'Well, say so, an' don't make them out to be ancient before their time.'

'Sorry.'

If it could be said that Gerald knew everything there was to be known about his Rudge Whitworth, then it could equally be said that Miriam knew everything there was to be known about Gerald; she even knew the order of priority of his late afternoon programme: the Rudge first, his homework second, and supper with his parents third; but she had deliberately shuffled the predetermined sequence purely for conversation's sake.

She was employed as the Mansons' cook about a month after Gerald was born, and, over the years, she had earned the indisputable right, not only to be their companion and confidante but also to be Gerald's guardian and mentor.

'Got you' t'ings for the Rudge?' she asked.

'In the tool-bag under the saddle, as usual.'

'As usual,' she said dryly.

Gerald began to move towards his bedroom door.

'Shoes, please,' she said, pointing to the badly dented rubber-and-wire mat on the landing of the veranda steps. 'Wipe off the school-yard.'

Gerald did so, briskly, perhaps excessively, which made Miriam say, 'Enough's as good as a hole in the sole.'

14

He shrugged and carried on, if only to counter her gentle, though effective, mocking attempt to put him in his place.

'You can stop now,' she said mildly, 'an' mind the bedroom floor; I jus' finish' polishin' it.'

He smiled and tiptoed into his room.

She chuckled softly and padded slowly back to her kitchen. She was happy now that Gerald had come in; ever since his father had given him the scholarship Rudge, Miriam had become increasingly concerned about his bicycle-riding, especially during the rush-hour periods in the morning and late afternoon, and particularly in the company of Shifty and Fu, whom she often called, despairingly, 'Satan' pickney'.

3

Gerald was standing beside his bed and looking down at the front page of the *Gleaner*, which, he thought, Miriam may have left there after she had done her mid-morning cleaning.

He read:

OPERATIONS BEGIN AT BROOME SUGAR ESTATE

The Windies Sugar Corporation began operations earlier this week. The news has, so far, proved to be both promising and gloomy, simply because only a handful of workers can be employed, and the bulk of applicants will have to be turned away.

The reason for such cold comfort, in an otherwise welcome event of industrial news, is the fact that there are just not enough jobs to go round at Broome. This new source of easing the general pressure of unemployment is bound to satisfy only a very few of the out-of-work casual labourers but it will not be able to meet the demands of the larger percentage of the hopeful thousands who, over the past months, have been seeking employment, not only in the sugar industry but also in the other industrial enterprises in the rural areas.

Gerald folded the paper, took it to the sitting-room and put it down on the seat of his father's armchair. Then he went back to his bedroom and changed into his 'house clothes' which, he knew, Miriam expected him to do before going out to clean his bicycle.

He had just slipped on his khaki short trousers and was about to put on his shirt when he heard Miriam say, 'I saw you readin' the paper. Wha' was occupyin' you so?'

'The bit about Broome,' he said, turning from her modestly and buttoning up his khaki sports shirt.

'I was readin' it this mornin' meself,' she said slowly, her voice sounding deeper and more solemn than usual. 'This Broome business is bad business. A promise mus' be a promise, come hell or high water. Half measure cause' heartburn.'

'Has Dad seen it?'

'Boun' to. From early this mornin'.'

'Did he say anything?'

'Wha' you' father can say, Gerry? He don't even 'ave a proper Union behin' 'im to fall back on.'

'What d'you mean by a "proper" Union?'

'The t'ing he callin' the C.I.T.U. is not a proper Union until it register itself as such in a proper legal way, Gerry. Right now it only exis' in Crossman' head an' in you' father' mind an' in the dreams o' few other intelligent workin' people in Kingston.'

'But why? Dad's always talking about it. Why hasn't it been established?'

'Simple reason, son. You mus' know how hard it is for black people to believe in anyt'ing that black people want to set up in this country? We don't 'ave any respec' for one another an' that is our downfall.'

Gerald muttered something to make her know that he had heard her little speech of anguish and protest, but he had not really understood it. He smiled and left the room. On the way out to the back-yard, he stopped in at the kitchen, sniffed the overheated air, which was charged with Miriam's cooking, rummaged in a cupboard drawer for a damp cloth which he knew she usually kept in reserve for him, found it, sniffed appreciatively again, and ran out of the kitchen before she could catch up with him.

He wiped the dust off the metal parts of the Rudge, turned the bicycle upside-down and rested it on the saddle and handlebar, and began to clean the spokes and the rims of the wheels. He spent a fairly long time doing that. Later on, when he was oiling the teeth of the ratchet, he sensed the presence of someone standing over him; he turned, looked up and saw a tall man wearing a Panama hat and dressed in a white drill suit, with white boots.

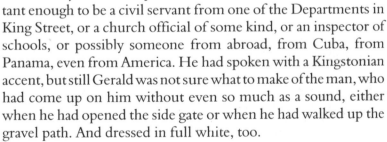

'Your father in, son?' the man asked.

'Hasn't come in yet,' Gerald said respectfully, very nearly standing at attention as he spoke and wondering who the man was.

As far as Gerald could see, he certainly looked impor-tant enough to be a civil servant from one of the Departments in King Street, or a church official of some kind, or an inspector of schools, or possibly someone from abroad, from Cuba, from Panama, even from America. He had spoken with a Kingstonian accent, but still Gerald was not sure what to make of the man, who had come up on him without even so much as a sound, either when he had opened the side gate or when he had walked up the gravel path. And dressed in full white, too.

'D'you know when he'll be in?' the man asked.

'Dad's usually back from the foundry by six on Fridays.'

'Half an hour to go then,' the man said, after he had looked at his wrist watch. It was large, gold-plated, and very impressive, and it had a broad, gold 'metal-elastic' band which he tugged a few times; after each tug, it *flip-flopped* tightly round his wrist.

'Did you buy your watch downtown?' Gerald asked, utterly embarrassed by the sudden familiarity and pointedness of his question but completely incapable of checking the compulsion of his curiosity.

'No, son,' the man said. 'England. In a shop in London. As a matter of fact, your father bought one exactly like mine but it was stolen. In London.'

'You know my Dad then?'

'I've known him for many years.'

'So you're not from abroad?'

'No. But I've been abroad often enough.'

'Are you going to wait until he gets in?'

'No. I'll come back later tonight.'

The man spun the front wheel of the Rudge and then the back wheel, and he listened for the approved 'soft' sounds of professional tuning and oiling, and he also listened for the 'purring' of the centre pin in the sprocket, and when he heard them he smiled and said, 'Good condition. Can't beat oiled wheels.'

Gerald watched him closely as he walked down to the side gate and recalled how similar the man's height and bearing and slightly rolling walk were to his own father's. The one remarkable difference was the fact that his father never wore white, except for his traditional white shirt on Sundays and on very special occasions.

The man wove himself slowly, and with stalking dignity, in and out of the up-and-down streams of cars and trucks and buses along Half Way Tree Road, and when he got to the far side, he turned and waved. Gerald waved back, then hugged the top of the gate and rested his chin on his forearms, and stared at the man in silent wonder: there he was, the white-clad stranger in town, passing the Movies cinema, Sloppy Joe's, the Chinese Restaurant, heading towards the sunset beyond Cross Roads, taking in everything around him, quick on the draw if absolutely necessary, and with only one friend in town who was not around at the moment; and of course, there they were, the townspeople, the tavern-keeper, the dry-goods clerk, the butcher's assistant, the pedlars, the wealthy merchants, the strollers, the idlers, the troublemakers, riding confidently past him on their horses and not knowing that the law man was in their midst.

Gerald waited until the receding white form of the man's clothes became a thin chalk line against the blackboard clutter of the pedestrians on the pavement in front of the Bata Store, and until the white slit faded out of sight.

He went back to the Rudge and spun the front wheel, and then the back one, and while standing back from them with a self-congratulatory smile, he suddenly remembered that he had not asked the man his name.

CHAPTER TWO

1

At about five forty-five, Gerald's father walked wearily through the half-open, zinc-panelled, wooden double-doors of the Kingston Foundry, and was confronted by a deputation of workers. Martin Manson's face showed obvious signs of stress.

Marcus Johnson, an apprentice, stepped forward and asked, 'Wha' the plan, Missa Manson?' The young man spoke with a slight stutter, and his shoulders drooped with the accumulated exhaustion of the harassing working week. His face was haggard and stained with sweat and grime.

Martin Manson spread his arms wide to take in the deputation and then he pointed to the foundry gate. They understood his unspoken order and they walked slowly, trustingly, with hunched shoulders and dangling arms, behind him. Their heavy boots crunched the pebbles on the paved surface of the yard and their marching footsteps echoed long and hard like hammers cracking chunks of sheet glass.

Outside, they gathered round Martin Manson and waited. The tension was evident. 'You know about the situation at Broome?' he asked them.

They nodded and shifted uneasily.

'Well,' he continued, 'we'll have to come out. No other course of action.'

'When?' Marcus asked.

Martin stared at him, and then he glanced at the other faces round him. He felt his responsibility nagging at his confidence, pushing it forward, hurling him into a position of leadership which made him feel both anxious and courageous. He wanted to go out and prove himself and at the same time he wanted to hold back and check and double-check his position, his advice, his proposals.

He glanced again at their faces and recalled the misery of their working conditions, the dejection in which they and their families and he and his had to live, the hopelessness of their struggle and of his.

He felt the weight, the terrible dead weight of their dependence pressing in on him. Their eyes told their story. They stared at him, claiming him, trusting him, and waiting for him to lead the way.

'When, Missa Manson?' Marcus asked again.

Martin sighed quietly, smiled easily and said, 'I'll know for certain as soon as I've spoken to Crossman. He promised to come to see me at home. Might be waiting there now.'

The men nodded again.

Then there was a short discussion of matters relating to procedure and action, followed by a few words about the approach to the management of the foundry. Before they broke up, Martin said, 'We meet tomorrow morning early. Six o'clock. Outside here.'

They walked away, gesturing limply, and muttering among themselves.

Martin was left alone with the urgency of his thoughts. His men were not the only ones waiting for his decision; the Kingston dockers were also waiting to take their lead from the action of the foundry workers. And waiting, too, in their turn, were the others from the ice company, the match factory, the slaughter house, the Kingston and Saint Andrew bus company, and the rest of the workers in the light industrial jobs in the corporate area and in certain sections of the outlying districts beyond the city.

Martin turned round and faced the foundry yard. He cast his tired, grit-filled eyes over the hard grey litter which was spread out in front of him; he noticed the usual tiny mounds of iron filings, the ant-hills of rusting coil springs, the odd lengths of piping, the abandoned crowbars, nails, and wire-matting. He closed his eyelids, squeezed his knuckles into them and flooded his eyeballs with tears. Then he opened his eyes and wiped the moist corners with his brown calico handkerchief.

Suddenly he remembered that he ought to make some sort of an approach to the management concerning the intention of the foundry workers to stage a token sympathy strike to register their protest against the failure at Broome and to warn the foundry Board that they intended to draw further attention to their own working conditions and wages and general discontent. He went back inside and asked the foreman to contact the managing director's office about an interview, either on the spot in a matter of minutes, or early the following day.

He got his reply almost seconds after the foreman had put through his telephone call to the managing director's office. The foreman replaced the receiver on the cradle of the telephone-stand, smiled spitefully and said to Martin, 'He sen' to tell you that you an' you' sympathy strike an' you' discontent an' you' so-call' Union can go an' play hopscotch in the foundry yard 'til hell freeze over fifty times.'

Martin thanked the foreman sardonically and set out for the bus-stop a few streets away. On the way, he passed through the familiar working-class back alleys with their bleached, ramshackle frontages; he stared at the clusters of defeated, poverty-stricken people lining the dusty front yards, at the unemployed men and their brooding wives, standing and leaning about the place, at the older men and women with their arms folded in resignation and their eyes lowered hopelessly; and he stood and watched the ragged children improvising their noisy regattas with paper boats in the narrow, fetid gutters.

Martin thought immediately of Gerald, and of Gerald's two close friends, Shifty and Fu, and he turned away from the playing children.

A wave of bitterness and resentment swept over him, and he shook with suppressed rage. He mumbled something to himself and quickly stifled a cry of indignation.

Just as he was about to move away, an old woman, who had been watching him closely, tapped her stick briskly on the railing of a low wooden fence and called out, 'The young people waitin' for the Union, Missa Manson; we ol' ones waitin' for a bigger miracle.' And she laughed a dry, raucous, old woman's laugh of self-mockery.

2

Martin arrived home at six-thirty. Jessica, his wife, had got in a little before him, and had prepared a table and two chairs in a corner of the sitting-room for his meeting with Alexander Crossman. On the table she had placed two small note-pads, two newly sharpened H.B. pencils, the *Gleaner* and the exercise-book in which Martin and Crossman had been jotting down scraps of information about the final shape of the C.I.T.U.

Jessica Manson had been neat and precise in laying the table; she had seen to everything as if she had been preparing for one of her classes at school.

Gerald had been conveniently excluded from her preparations; he had been put to sit at the dining-table on the back veranda where he always did his homework.

23

His father had passed behind his chair when he came in, and had patted his head roughly, in his own affectionate manner, and in silent approval.

Gerald was on the last paragraph of his English composition. When that was finished, his homework would all be done, and then supper. But he suddenly remembered the man in white. He got up and went in search of his father. He found him talking to his mother on the front veranda. When they saw him approaching, they stopped their conversation and turned stonily towards him.

He knew that he was interrupting something very special between his parents; ordinarily they would have asked him what he wanted, but this time they merely stared at him and waited. They were tense and on the verge of impatience.

'A man came to see you this afternoon, Dad,' Gerald began tentatively. 'He said he knew you.'

'What's his name, Gerry?' Martin asked.

'Didn't ask.'

'You *didn't*?'

'Didn't.'

'Why didn't you, Gerry?'

'Forgot.'

'You're going to *forget* once too often, Gerry,' Jessica teased him, cutting across the mounting anger of her husband. 'What did he look like?'

'He was dressed in white,' Gerald told her. 'All in white. And tall. And he said that he has known Dad for many years, a long time. And he had a gold watch. Like the one you bought in England, Dad. The one which was stolen.' He was rather proud of having reported the last fact; it made him feel 'included', particularly close to his father for the moment, very important indeed.

Martin smiled. Jessica relaxed.

'When did he come?' she asked.

'About five-thirty,' Gerald said confidently.

'Did he say he was coming back later?' Martin asked.

'So he said.'

'Thanks, Gerry. Finished your homework?'

'Almost, Dad.'

'Finish it and we'll eat right after. O.K.?' Martin's change of mood was personally reassuring to Gerald. It gave him enough extra confidence to want to ask the question which was nagging him.

'What's the man's name, Dad?'

'Can't you guess?'

'No.'

'Never seen him before?'

'No.'

'Never seen him here before?'

'No.'

'He's been here a few times recently, Gerry,' Jessica said, 'but usually when you're in bed. Maybe that's why you didn't recognize him.'

'Maybe,' Gerald said a little offhandedly. 'Anyway, what's his name, Dad?'

'Crossman. Alexander Crossman.'

'Who's he?'

'The man in the white suit,' Martin taunted him.

'I know that. But what else?'

'The man with the gold watch.'

'Come on, Dad,' Gerald begged.

'Tell the boy, Martin,' Jessica said, laughing sympathetically.

'Alexander Crossman is the Union leader, Gerry. He started the business of the C.I.T.U., the idea of setting up a Union, and together we're trying to knock it into shape.'

Gerald nodded, hesitated, remembered what Miriam had said about his father and Crossman and the Union, hesitated again, and then said, 'I'd better finish the composition. See you, Dad.'

As soon as he had left, Martin and Jessica resumed their conversation. They talked for about twenty minutes.

Later on at the supper table, Gerald asked, 'Why isn't the Union established yet, Dad?'

Martin harpooned an enormous potato in its jacket, lifted it carefully, dropped it into a stream of hot butter in his plate and pretended that he had not heard his son's extremely pointed question.

Jessica was good at coping with situations which called for gentle dissuasion, even gentle evasion, but she was caught out this time. She looked at Martin and then at the large potato which she knew he really did not want. 'Look, Gerry,' she intervened, 'your father'll be talking nothing but Union affairs all night tonight; give him a break to take his mind off it at supper, eh.'

'How's school, Gerry?' Martin mustered enough courage to ask.

'School's all right.'

'And the Rudge?'

'All right.'

And that was that. But Martin felt uneasy. He felt embarrassed. He wished he had been able to say to Gerald, 'Yes, son, the Union will be officially established next week, or next month, or very, very soon.' But he couldn't. He and Alexander Crossman were no more than two over-enthusiastic gamblers, merely playing at a game of earnest 'make-believe'. The C.I.T.U. was still a matter of random jottings on pieces of notepaper. Some of the workers in Kingston were also caught up in the aura of the 'make-believe'. They had heard Crossman speak in the park at Parade and in the Race Course, and they had been impressed, but that was all. Crossman had gone no farther. He was still working out the details of the Union and testing the interest and loyalty of its potential working members. He and Martin were doubtful about attracting a large enough membership to make the Union a working reality. Most of the employed men and women whom they had met and spoken to personally and openly were suspicious and nervous about the plan. Some felt that, if they joined it, they would be automatically dismissed from their jobs, and some felt that they did not need a Union, while the rest were just plainly apathetic and withdrawn. Martin's only consolation was the fact that Jessica, Crossman, and a handful of his foundry friends had shown that they were wholly in favour of the Union. Crossman's consolation was simply that the society *needed* one, and that the working people in the society were inevitably going to get one. Both Martin and Crossman had seen for themselves, while they were on shore leave in London and Liverpool, during their years on the *Jamaica Commerce*, just how basically important and useful trades unions were, not only as protective agencies for the workers themselves but also for the benefit of the progress of commerce and industry as a whole. They had read about the work of the various Unions, about their dynamic representation, their powerful influence, and they had seen the results in the lives of the English working class. The memory of having read and seen all this in England had so impressed them that, now, in spite of their confusion and disappointments and the frustration of their own efforts, they were able to look back in one glance and gather enough moral strength to plan for the future, come what may.

3

After supper, Gerald slipped away from the numbing leisuredness of his parents' table-talk, and from Miriam's policing gaze, and went first to Shifty's fence and then to Fu's and whistled them both with the accustomed:

> *John to-wit*
> *Sweet John.*

They met in a huddle under an avocado-pear tree in Gerald's back garden.

'Thought you'd never whistle us over,' Shifty said to Gerald.

'Late supper, man,' Gerald explained.

'What's doing then?' Fu asked.

Gerald nudged him and said, 'By the way, Fu, how did you make out with ol' Grammar Book Weller?'

'Ol' Weller's a word-merchant,' Fu said with all the disrespect he could summon. 'Wants everybody to swallow the grammar book whole like him and spout Analysis and Parsing all over the place like a firs'-class jackass.'

'But not you, eh, Fu?' Gerald taunted gently.

'You know, boy,' Fu said. 'You know.'

'How about track, Shifty?' Gerald asked.

'There, Gerry,' Shifty said. 'Still there.'

'So what's doing tonight then?' Fu asked.

'Nothing,' Gerald said.

Shifty leapt up and did a series of 'knee-lifts' and 'overarm swings'. Then he said breathlessly, 'What about a ride up to Papine? Quick sprint up and cruise back down?'

'Now or later on?' Fu asked.

'Can you two get away, though?' Gerald asked before Shifty could reply.

'Suppose so,' Fu said.

Shifty nodded.

'We can go now if you want,' Gerald said. 'I'm dead easy.'

'How come?' Fu asked.

'Union business.'

'Your old man's still working on that?' Shifty asked.

'Big meeting tonight with the head man.'

'Who's that when he's at home?' Fu asked.

'Crossman. Alexander Crossman.'

'Mister White Suit himself,' Shifty said.

Gerald nodded.

'See him a mile off,' Fu said when he discovered whom they were talking about. 'Roun' town all the time. Some of the boys call him "Summertime"!' He chuckled.

'Dad's always talking about him,' Shifty said.

'Same here,' Fu added.

'So what're Crossman and your old man planning then, Gerry?' Shifty asked.

'Dunno really,' Gerald said. 'Something to do with the Broome business, maybe.'

'Saw it in the paper this morning,' Shifty said.

'Broome, *voom!*' Fu jeered. 'What about Papine?'

'Last Rudge out is a load o' scrap-iron!' Gerald shouted, and quickly raised his hand to his mouth with regret.

'Watchdog Miriam's bound to be on you' tail now, boy,' Fu said, and ran off.

Shifty took a running jump and cleared Gerald's side fence in an effortless Western Roll, and landed like a cat in his own back-yard.

Alexander Crossman came by taxi at a little after ten o'clock. His white suit was soiled and crushed and torn. He saw the sudden concern on the Mansons' faces as they stood to welcome him on the top step of their front veranda, so he volunteered the information which, he knew, would give meaning to everything that he and Martin had been planning. 'It's started, Martin and Jessica,' he explained. 'The upheaval's come at last.'

'Where?' Jessica asked, taking hold of his elbow and leading him to the nearest of the eight Berbice chairs on the veranda.

'It's started at Broome.'

'How d'you know for certain, Alex?' Martin asked. 'You haven't been out there? You couldn't have gone out there and come back already?'

'No,' Crossman said, breathing deeply and trying to control his own excitement, 'I haven't. I heard the news at the Cable and Wireless office a while ago, before coming up to you.'

'What did the news say?' Jessica asked.

'Insufficient work to go round at Broome,' Crossman began less excitedly. 'No promise of better prospects. Too many applications. Hundreds locked out this morning. Heated talk. Police sent for. Resistance. Riot broke out. Panic. Police brutality. And now the rioting is spreading.'

'Where to?' Martin asked.

'In and around Broome,' Crossman said, completely calmly now. 'Things happen slowly in the rural areas, as you know, but they *happen*, even if they take a longer time than they would in Kingston. The rioting is supposed to be spreading from one estate to the next in the Broome vicinity, according to the last report I was listening to downtown.'

'What happened to your clothes?' Jessica asked.

'There was a little scuffle in sympathy at the Cable office,' he said casually.

'In sympathy?' she said. 'But why against you?'

'Not against me, Jessica. I just got caught up in it. It was actually against the night-duty clerks and supervisors in the office. You know how that sort of thing can happen.'

'But why?' Martin asked.

'Irrational,' Crossman said, 'but to be expected.'

'An easy target,' Jessica suggested.

'Anything or anybody in sight, within easy reach, will do, when news of that sort gets around,' Crossman said. 'A few dockers were standing in the street when the report came in and they took it out on the Cable office building before you could say "Jack Robinson".'

'And that's when you got roughed up?' Jessica asked.

'I tried to stop them, stupidly enough as it may seem to you.'

'We've got to think this one out, Alex,' Martin said seriously, looking at Crossman's suit and counting the large bloodstains on the lapels of his jacket. 'Did you get badly beaten up?'

'Don't think so. Though I did get in the way of a few stray fists and stones, but that's all.'

'Were you trying to stop the dockers?'

'Didn't want them to get into trouble, Martin.'

'Might work against us, you mean?'

'Just that.'

The two men fell silent. Jessica stood and said, 'I'll get you a cloth and warm water to clean up, and something to eat.'

Crossman nodded.

Jessica then turned to Martin and said, 'Seems funny that the Broome employment intake should've sparked off the violence.'

'Too few jobs can be worse than no jobs at all, Jessy,' Martin reminded her.

'Now that the ball's rolling,' Crossman added, 'we've got to break in and get it under our control, Martin, as soon as we can. But how?'

'We'll figure something out later on,' Martin told him.

'We'd better. So far, the riot is leaderless. If we can hold on to the ball, it could mean the beginning of the establishment of the Union.'

'It could at that,' Martin said cautiously. 'It could.'

At midnight, Marcus Johnson, the apprentice at the Kingston Foundry, knocked at Martin Manson's front gate. Martin called out and told him to come in.

Marcus, who had been riding, leant the borrowed bicycle on the fence and ran up to the veranda and said breathlessly, 'You all hear wha' 'appenin' out by Broome?'

Jessica, Martin and Crossman nodded.

'Well,' Marcus continued, 'it' worse now. The Broome factory buildin', the new one, been broken open an' fire been set right inside it; the canefields on either side o' the road blazin' too; six o' the men on the outside been killed; twenty police constables an' specials in 'ospital; an' the complete, entire countryside marchin' on Broome an' on the other estates in the parish.'

'That's the very latest?' Crossman asked.

'From Cable an' Wireless, yes,' Marcus said.

'Any signs of trouble downtown?' Martin asked.

'Not now,' Marcus said. 'Mos' people don't know anyt'ing yet 'bout the Broome riot. They sleepin' anyway.'

'Any more disturbances at the Cable office?' Jessica asked.

'You heard 'bout that, too?' Marcus said.

Jessica inclined her head towards Crossman and said, 'He was there.'

Marcus nodded quickly and blinked. Then he said, 'No more disturbance'. The police outside the buildin' an' the dockers gone away for the time bein', I suppose.'

Jessica left to make coffee and sandwiches for Marcus, and to look in on Gerald to see if he was sleeping; she suspected that he may have been listening in, all the time, from a safe distance somewhere at the back of the sitting-room. But there were no signs in his bedroom to show that he had been up; his shirt and trousers were hanging over the top of his bedroom chair and he was covered up to his waist by the thin cotton sheet. His polished shoes were on his shoe-rack and his slippers were at his bedside where she had last seen them when he had got into bed.

When Jessica got to the kitchen, she ran into Miriam who had been fixing herself a mug of bush tea.

'Can't sleep, don't care how I try,' was her simple explanation to Jessica.

'What's wrong, Miriam?'

'I jus' feel, in my bones, that somet'ing not right tonight. That's all.'

'Like what for instance?'

'Like wha' you an' Missa Martin an' Missa Crossman talkin' 'bout on the front veranda.'

'You've been listening, Miriam,' Jessica teased her.

'Concern me, too, Miss Jessy.'

'Concerns us all, Miriam.'

'Well, then?'

Miriam's 'Well, then?' was enough for Jessica; she knew its implication. Miriam had her own inimitable way of cutting off all possible exchange between herself and another speaker with those magically curt, final words. And so, there was nothing to be done about it. But Miriam felt a little pity for her employer and for the men on the veranda, who were, she was certain, genuinely concerned about her welfare and about the welfare of the mass of the people like herself.

'I fix wha' you want,' she said to Jessica, and smiled.

'Some sandwiches and coffee, Miriam, and come and sit with us, if you want to,' Jessica said, and left the kitchen.

She decided not to walk back through the house to the front veranda but to go by way of the side yard.

The heat was stifling and appropriately close for the time of the year. Flaming June's just round the corner, she reminded herself, and flaming days ahead, possibly. She bent and touched the firm, red skin of a large salad tomato which was hanging from a low growth of leaves, propped up by a makeshift espalier; she cleared a few wilting leaves away from the espalier and powdered a clump of dry ones near the tomato and dropped them at the root of the

32

growth to form the basis of a mulch heap. She walked on, brushing the traces of the leaves off her fingers and looking around her at the small vegetable garden, at the experimental bed of watercress and inhaling the perfume of the jasmine growing along the border of the side fence. Then her thoughts came back to the crisis, to her husband's part in it, to Crossman and the Union, and with a jolt, to everybody's safety.

She told herself that Gerald had better not go out on the Rudge, not go out at all for that matter. She was convinced that the rioting was bound to spread to Kingston. It would occur in bursts at first, here and there, in the streets, in people's houses, anywhere. And then it would become intensified in a given area and spread out in a concentrated stream, to Cross Roads, Half Way Tree, and into Upper Saint Andrew. She was very worried suddenly.

What would Martin do in all this? What would he and Crossman feel called upon to do because of the Union? Surely they would want to go out into the thick of it? They would want to make immediate use of the upheaval to promote their idea of a meaningful Union later on. But it would be dreadfully dangerous. They might get injured, arrested, killed. How would their death serve the Union? It wouldn't. There wouldn't be anybody to take over from them. They must be careful. But they will want to expose themselves. They *will*. They'll *have* to. No other way. That's the whole idea of using the upheaval for their own end. But Martin will have to be careful. He *must* be. For Gerald's sake. For the sake of the Union. For Crossman's sake. For the sake of the dream they've both shared for so long, for so very long. Perhaps they'll only be arrested.

She got to the front veranda in time to hear Marcus asking, 'An' wha' 'bout the Kingston end o' the operation, Missa Manson?'

'The upheaval, the violence, the impetus, call it what you will, the energy, has got to come to Kingston first, Marcus, if it's to make any sense at all,' Martin said thoughtfully, slowly, counting his words and giving them a certain dramatic edge.

'It will,' Crossman said. 'And if it doesn't, we've got to see to it that it does.'

'Aren't we asking for trouble, Alex?' Jessica said nervously. 'Big trouble?'

'We're asking for a Union, Jessica,' Crossman said. 'We're asking for a break, an attention-drawing device.'

'The kind we might all regret?' she suggested with a wry chuckle. 'The kind we won't be able to see the end of in all probability?'

'We've got to take that chance,' Martin intervened.

Jessica sat down and stared into the midnight grey of Half Way Tree Road and waited for Miriam to bring out Marcus's snack.

'By the way,' Martin said bleakly, 'the Foundry management won't see us. Refused bluntly.'

Crossman shrugged. Marcus smiled. Jessica closed her eyes.

'We still meet at six o'clock tomorrow?' Marcus asked Martin.

'Six o'clock *today*, this morning,' Martin corrected.'

'Yes,' Marcus said, grinning self-consciously. 'Saturday a'ready.'

'The *riot* already,' Crossman said, as if reminding himself of the fact.

'We've always wanted a change, Alex,' Martin said, 'and we've got it coming.'

CHAPTER THREE

1

Martin Manson got out of bed shortly before five o'clock on Saturday morning He had not slept well; he had had a morning of fitful sleep during which he had been tormented by a number of recurring childhood nightmares: first, he found himself sitting at a very long, low mahogany dining-table, laden with watermelon slices, and trying desperately to get at them but not being able to touch even the nearest slice; then, he became entangled in a giant spiral of barbed wire, leading nowhere in particular; and finally, he was walking across the deep water of Kingston Harbour, which licked at his ankles for a time then sucked him in whole and spat him out again as he tried to reach Victoria Pier.

He tiptoed out of the bedroom and went straight to the shower-bath at the back of the house; he felt that he needed a shower to help him to dispel his depression which had been brought on by his nightmares; he always relied on an early morning shower and it had never failed him. Gerald, too, imitated him in this and found it a cure-all for his usual late-rising and general disinclination about setting off for school.

But for Martin, the water was hardly cold enough; yet, even though it was not as refreshing as he had expected, the force of the jet-sprays pounded his body and broke the spell of his mental fatigue and his despondency.

Miriam had heard him bathing and had fixed his usual mug of steaming Blue Mountain coffee with 'coolie foot' sugar. While he was sipping it, Gerald crept up behind him and waited until he could summon the courage to speak. He knew that his father would want to send him back to bed and that that would obviously spoil his plan. But his heavy breathing betrayed him.

'That you, Gerry?' Martin asked without turning round.

'Yes,' Gerald said, almost in an apologetic whisper.

'What're you doing up so early?'

Gerald breathed in deeply and decided to come to the point straight away. 'Can I come with you as far as the foundry gate?'

'Why?'

' 'Cause I want to, Dad. No school today. Besides, something's going on, somewhere. Isn't there?'

Martin told him about the news at Broome and about the incident at the Cable and Wireless office, and asked, 'What made you suspect?'

'Heard the voices on the veranda every time I woke up last night, Dad.'

'Your mother, Crossman and Marcus Johnson from the Foundry,' Martin explained.

'I know. I caught the voices but not what they were saying.'

Martin knew that he had to avoid the obvious direct reply to Gerald's statement, so he said, 'Taking the Rudge with you?'

'Yes.'

'I'll walk, I think. Early enough.'

'We've got lots of time, Dad. I can coast beside you.'

'You just make sure you get back home before your mother wakes up.'

'Ages before, Dad.' Then he suddenly remembered Shifty and Fu. He looked at his father to see how receptive he would be to his urgent request.

'What're you looking at?' Martin asked.

'Nothing,' Gerald said.

'Something else on your mind?'

Gerald faltered.

'Come on, out with it, Gerry. What is it?'

'Can Shifty and Fu come with us?'

'Will you take the responsibility when their parents start asking questions?'

'It'll be all right, Dad. We'll be back before they get up.'

Miriam shuffled past the dining-table and sighed her ancient sigh of disapproval at their conspiracy, every word of which she had been listening to attentively at the sink in the kitchen.

Gerald thought that he would hit back mock-defiantly at her sigh by letting her know that he had also heard her voice on the veranda along with the others. He calculated that, by doing so, he would prove that he had had her 'covered' without her knowing, but he thought better of his scheme and forgot it. But she had noticed the glint of attack in his eye and she said in passing, 'The Devil can find plenty botheration for those with idle hands.' She paused, chuckled knowingly, and added, 'An' big ears!'

To which Martin, the unchallenged conspirator in the case, said, 'Very true, Miriam. Very true.' And he winked at Gerald.

2

Cross Roads looked like the mysterious town-centre in a deserted Dodge City to Gerald, Shifty and Fu: no traffic, no policemen, no passers-by except two butchers in their white aprons on their way to the meat market and a newspaper boy on his bicycle, and no sounds except the occasional arrogant blast of a rooster somewhere along Old Hope Road.

Martin stopped the newspaper boy and bought a copy of the *Gleaner*.

Gerald, Shifty and Fu parked their Rudges in front of Nelson's Drug Store and sat on the crossbars and listened while Martin read out the reports of the scenes at Broome and at the Cable and Wireless office. He also read out the report of an incident of provocation which had taken place on the building site of a Kingston housing scheme, where the labourers who had been working on the project had been jeered at and stoned by a crowd of unemployed men; this had happened late on Friday afternoon immediately after the building workers had been paid.

'Crossman didn't tell me about this,' Martin said. He looked away from the paper and stared at the highly polished surface of the front fenders of the three Rudges.

'Maybe he didn't know,' Gerald said.

'Maybe.'

'So what does it mean, Mr. Manson?' Shifty asked.

'Trouble, son. Big trouble.'

They moved off slowly together, Gerald leading his bicycle with one hand resting on the saddle, the other in his side-pocket, and his father walking beside him; Shifty and Fu followed behind them. They walked down Slipe Road and when they came to Torrington Bridge, Gerald told Martin to sit on the crossbar of his bicycle.

'It's downhill, Dad,' he said, 'and there isn't any traffic. I'll tow you the rest of the way to the foundry.'

'Suppose a "pan head" policeman spots us?'

'No "pan head" can catch the Rudge on a downgrade, no time at all,' Gerald boasted.

'Been chased before, eh?' Martin tried to trap him.

'No. Just know. That's all.'

Shifty and Fu grinned broadly.

Martin accepted Gerald's invitation and allowed himself to be towed down to the foundry.

When they got there, they saw two hunched figures sitting on the parapet along the front fence. One was an old machinist and the other was Marcus Johnson.

'Early for six,' Martin said, smiling at Marcus. 'Slept out here this morning?'

Marcus laughed and got up and brushed the seat of his grease-stained khaki trousers. The machinist sat where he was and admired the boys' bicycles. The boys showed they were flattered.

'So, what about the business on the building site?' Martin asked both men, with a curious mixture of apprehension and approval showing through the casualness of his question.

'T'ings revvin' up,' Marcus said jubilantly. 'Saw it in today's paper.' He patted his *Gleaner* which was folded neatly in his back-pocket.

'A little bit o' provokin' can work magic sometimes,' the machinist said, getting up to join them.

Gerald, Shifty and Fu sat on the parapet and watched the men moving about restlessly; Shifty thought they looked like Championship athletes before *the* event.

The boys listened to the men's nervous bursts of chatter and they willed themselves to be a part of their world for as long as Martin would allow them to be there. But the boys knew that they were being excluded. They wanted to contribute to the discussion which seemed to be taking shape out of the men's conversation. They wanted to enter it as active participants. But how could they? They didn't know enough for that. They had not been expected to know, or expected to want to know. But Gerald knew he did want to know; his father's position in what was going on was sufficient incentive. The feeling of protest and violence in the air and in the gestures of the men, backed up by the evidence of the late-night meeting on his veranda at home and the reports in the *Gleaner*, was something else that pointed Gerald's interest towards engagement and participation. He was quite certain now that the upheaval, of which his father had always spoken, had begun and would continue, possibly for a week, for a month, even for a much longer time, and if it did go on, he felt that the excitement would involve him whether his father would want it to or not. So, why not get into it from the start?

But he did nothing about it. He listened, and so did Shifty and Fu. Secretly, they were scared of the coming violence.

Dawn was breaking with a warm, yellow crispness. The west end of Kingston, at that hour, was a simmering city within a city, with small groups of men getting awake with seething planless hopes for the day, with the old brand-mark of exploitation and abuse burning on their foreheads and along their limbs, with resentment and anger gnawing at their patience and sullen resignation: men dispossessed but moving towards a formless, leaderless revolt.

Fu touched Gerald's knee and said, 'Look over there at that man.' Shifty had heard him and he looked too.

An old beggar, dressed in filthy rags and with a dirty string of dented tin-cans slung over his right shoulder, was rooting in a heap of rubbish about fifty yards away. He was coughing and spitting frequently. His movements were jerky and menacing. His arms worked like short pistons and the tin cans clanked noisily.

'Don't you know who he is?' Gerald said. 'I know.'

Fu kept staring and did not reply. Neither did Shifty.

The beggar slipped and fell across the heap. He scrambled to his feet slowly and continued searching around the rim of the refuse.

'Haven't spotted him yet?' Gerald asked.

Fu shook his head. Shifty blinked.

Gerald smiled.

'Got it now,' Shifty said.

'Who?' Fu asked.

'It's that old man we see on North Street in front of school sometimes,' Shifty said.

' "Bag-'n'-Pan",' Gerald said.

'Straying far,' Fu said, laughing contemptuously.

'Nothing else for him to do,' Gerald observed coldly.

The beggar coughed and spat and sank to his knees with the exhaustion which the effort had inflicted. He collapsed soon afterwards and sprawled deep into the heap.

'Let's help him,' Gerald suggested.

'Got any pocket-money on you?' Shifty asked.

'I can spare a sixpence,' Fu said.

'I've got fourpence,' Gerald said.

'Thre'pence,' Shifty said, 'which is one-and-a-penny. Let's give it to him.'

They went over to the beggar and helped him up. Then Shifty offered him the small collection.

'Bag-'n'-Pan don't take money from chil'ren, t'ank you kin'ly,' the beggar said, waving aside Shifty's outstretched hand. He coughed and spat again and shuffled away from the boys and headed towards the pavement.

The boys were surprised and disappointed. They went back to the foundry fence, sat on the parapet and watched the old beggar moving painfully slowly down the street.

3

When Alexander Crossman arrived at the foundry gate, Martin felt it was time to send Gerald, Shifty and Fu home. It was twenty minutes to six. About thirty men had gathered. The boys left reluctantly. Before they rode away, Crossman walked over to Gerald and shook his hand vigorously. 'Look after your mother and lock up the house,' he warned. 'You can never tell. And ride safely.'

Martin said, 'Watch how you go, boys, and Gerry, you stay in today. I'll see you later.'

Gerald waved to his father and Crossman and to the gathering, and then he, Shifty and Fu mounted their bicycles with a run-hop-and-jump. As soon as they slid on to their saddles, they made a deliberate skidding noise with their back wheels in the style of a cycle-sports' sprint-start, and sped up the street.

On Gerald's suggestion, Shifty and Fu took two different routes to Cross Roads, and he, yet another.

Whenever he was riding alone, Gerald's Rudge *was* his 'iron horse'. He convinced himself that he was riding with a purpose; he was carrying an important message from the two divisional leaders of the rebel troops to a third across the expanse of enemy territory. He had to ride against time and against fate. The message had to be delivered before the stroke of six, and the messenger had to cross the vast, unpredictable areas of swampland, gully, savannah and jungle as if they were merely paved streets at dawn. And so he rode on fearlessly through the back-o'-wall neighbourhood of West Kingston, across to Parade, up Orange Street, to Torrington Bridge, and then he let go the reins of his 'horse', daring the snipers to shoot him down and inviting lesser risks, whatever they might be. Cruising along Slipe Road and emptying his mind of all concern and tension, he imagined he saw a gang of men, with broad, red armbands wrapped around their rolled-up shirt sleeves and with a look of defiance on their faces, coming at him from the opposite direction. He held the reins of his 'horse', spurred its 'flesh', and achieved a sudden acceleration. And just as suddenly, it seemed to Gerald that the men began converging in a rapidly closing inverted V, with the arms of the V pincering towards him. He felt the skin across his forehead becoming leathery and clammy with sweat, and the muscles along his forearms becoming elongated and hard. He kept going straight into the apex of the inverted V, and its arms continued to pincer steadily away from the pavements and close in towards the centre of the road. Why was there that look of defiance on their faces? he wondered. What did the red armbands stand for? And why were they moving like sleepwalkers? Why was the sound of their footsteps so even? So precise? And why were they converging on the 'iron horse'? Didn't they know that it would crash through their apex like a river stone from a sling-shot? He spurred the 'horse' again, hunched his shoulders, neatly tucked in his head turtle-style, and prepared to absorb the awful crescendo of the breakthrough. For a moment, he gritted his teeth and closed his eyes, and when he opened them, he found himself pelting headlong into the point-duty policeman's pedestal at the centre of Cross Roads. The menacing converging inverted V of red arm-banded, rolled-up shirt-sleeved men had faded into thin air and all that was left for Gerald to do was to cruise left into Half Way Tree Road and meet up with Shifty and Fu. But they had not yet arrived. So, instead of waiting around for them, he slipped quietly through the side gate and round to the back of his house and hoped that his mother had not got up during his absence. As he was walking up the steps of the back veranda, he heard the sitting-room wall-clock striking six o'clock.

4

Just at that moment, about a hundred-and-fifty workers had assembled at the front gate of the foundry, and were about to be addressed by Alexander Crossman.

Martin was standing on his right and Marcus Johnson was on his left.

Crossman began: 'The plan is simple; it's this: we've got to walk out of the foundry *today*, and when I say today, I mean this very minute. Not later today. Not this afternoon. Not after work. But now. Right now! In other words, from this moment, just where you're standing, you're *all* on strike!'

The men murmured their approval. They shifted their position but kept the overall shape of the gathering.

'Incidentally,' Martin told them, 'the management won't see us. We're on our own.'

Crossman shrugged his shoulders in mock-regret and smiled. Then he went on to speak about the absolute necessity of maintaining discipline and silence throughout the demonstration of

43

the walk-out. He also stressed the urgency of solidarity, loyalty and dignity.

After that, he returned to the actual moment of the strike. He said, 'Right here and right now!'

'We stan' outside 'ere?' Marcus asked, doubting the simplicity of Crossman's order.

'That's right, Marcus,' Crossman said. 'Right here by the gate.'

'Well,' Martin said, 'now that that is fixed, what's the plan for the others?'

'You and I'll go round and let them know what we've done here at the foundry, and offer to organize them, if they want us to.'

'Will it be as easy as that?'

'Why not? We're not strangers. They all know who we are and what we've been trying to do for them and for the Union.'

'Where do we start?' Martin asked more self-confidently.

'The nearest place to the foundry,' Crossman said, looking over the heads of the gathering towards the dock area, and then back at Martin.

'The dockers and casual wharf-labourers are the nearest,' Martin said, 'but d'you think they're ready for us?'

'When's *ready* ready?' Crossman laughed. 'You've got to make a start, ready or not ready.'

'O.K.,' Martin agreed. 'The dockyards.'

'Right. We'll start at Number Three Pier.'

Crossman and Martin left Marcus in charge of the men at the foundry gate and set out on their strike-action tour; their first stop was at the busiest of the Kingston wharves.

5

After Gerald, Shifty and Fu had made sure that everything was all right at their homes, they met under the avocado-pear tree.

Gerald decided not to tell Shifty and Fu about his hallucination on Slipe Road. But he had something to discuss with them. Before he began, he teased them both, 'You' need a jet-motor to catch up with me next time.'

'You must've taken the shortest route,' Shifty complained.

'If I know you, Gerry,' Fu said, 'you must've held on to the back of a bus.'

'That's more down your line, Fu,' Gerald countered. 'Anyway, I've got an idea.'

'About what?' Shifty asked.

'About the riot.'

'What're you talking about, Gerry, boy?' Fu demanded. There was the accustomed doubting ring in his voice.

'This whole thing of Broome and Crossman and Dad and the big trouble coming down to Kingston,' Gerald said, and then stopped to see what effect his introductory information had had.

'Go on, man,' Shifty urged. He was becoming interested. And Gerald knew that he obviously would be.

'How d'we figure, Gerry?' Fu sounded very doubtful.

'We've got to be in it,' Gerald said simply. 'Right in it.'

'In it?' Fu raised his voice.

'Yes. In it.' Gerald was cool.

'How?' Shifty asked.

'Well,' Gerald said, 'we've got to arrange to be around to see what happens.'

'Like going out into it while it's going on, you mean?' Fu asked.

'Right,' Gerald said.

'What about the old people?' Shifty asked. 'We've got to play it cool and dodge them, if we can get away with it.'

'Like how?' Fu was beginning to show some real interest in Gerald's proposal.

'Dunno yet,' Gerald said, 'but we've got to move together. Whenever the coast's clear for one of us, that person's got to contact the other two, and if they're *easy*, then we move.'

'Where to?' Fu asked.

'Depends on what's happening where,' Gerald pointed out.

'Seems all right by me,' Shifty agreed.

'O.K.,' from Fu.

'One thing,' Gerald said. 'We've got to promise not to rat on one another.'

'Fixed,' from Shifty.

'Same here,' from Fu.

'We've got to swear to it,' Gerald stressed.

'Swear?' Fu was caught off guard.

'Why?' Shifty asked.

'To make it *good*,' Gerald explained abruptly.

'Make what good!' Fu objected. 'We promised. We don't have to make anything *good*, after that.'

'It's really a sort of secret society thing we've got now,' Gerald said. 'And so far, we've only promised. We've got to swear and seal it.'

'Haven't got to,' Fu refused adamantly.

'No harm in it,' Shifty said.

'No harm,' Fu said; 'no need to swear then.'

Gerald ignored Fu and stood facing the avocado-pear tree. He tapped the trunk three times and mumbled a few words and afterwards cautioned Shifty to do the same.

Shifty said, 'O.K.' and did so swiftly and confidently.

Then Gerald waited for Fu to follow.

Fu pouted stubbornly, lowered his head thoughtfully and stretched out to touch the trunk of the tree, but stopped short.

'Go on!' Shifty shouted.

Fu hesitated. Then he did it.

'Great!' Gerald announced. 'We've got to stick together. No going back now.'

'What happens first?' Shifty asked.

'We find out what's going on, then we decide how to chip out and get next to it.'

'As easy as that?' Fu asked.

'It won't be easy,' Gerald warned. 'But we'll manage. O.K.?'

Shifty nodded. Fu grinned.

'Sure now?' Gerald asked.

Shifty nodded again, and Fu said, 'Tough lines. Anyway, I'm in.'

6

When Martin and Crossman got to the entrance of the Number Three Pier, they noticed immediately that there was something strange about the atmosphere of the dockyard; there was an unusual calm surrounding everything, a remarkable 'waiting' feeling hanging over the grey-and-iron rust of the dusty yard. There was, of course, a group of some thirty or forty dockers standing together and talking quietly. When they saw Martin and Crossman, they began walking slowly towards them, scuffing the straw and loose stones and disused light metal oddments in their path. They looked like condemned men, without hope, without direction, merely going through the process of seeming to be alive, moving but really heading nowhere. As they walked, their arms hung loosely and their heads dipped and sagged despondently with each step they took.

'My God!' Crossman thought compassionately as he watched them approaching the parking-lot on the left side of the entrance. Martin saw the look on his friend's face and recognized it for what it was; he, too, had been thinking how badly browbeaten the men looked.

Their leader came up to Crossman and saluted.

'We jus' decide, all o' us, to back up the 'appenin' at Broome, Missa Crossman,' he said formally. 'You got a plan for us?'

Crossman smiled. 'Yes. I've got a plan for all of us. Drop everything and walk out, as from now.'

'Easy t'ing that, Missa Crossman,' the man said. Then he turned to his men and ordered them off the premises. 'Out to the front, everybody! Slow an' no noise.'

'Can I depend on you for a peaceful demonstration?' Crossman asked.

'Tha's right,' the man replied and winked.

'What's the position with the bulk of the work on hand?' Martin asked him.

'Enough on the docks to kill an army, Missa Manson,' he said, smiling ironically.

'Perishable stuff in the cargo?'

'Tons.'

Martin nodded, and the man walked away.

Crossman looked round the dockyard and shook his head and said to Martin, 'Starvation wages, donkey hours, and no bargaining power – time for a change, Martin.'

All that Martin could say was, 'True.'

Both men bore their shame quietly, intensely, knowing only too well that their struggle had not even begun to make a mark on the conscience of the public or indeed on the compassion of those responsible for the intolerable conditions of the workers.

Martin and Crossman went on to Number Two Pier and farther on to Number One, and at each, all the men were ready and waiting to be told what to do.

Everywhere they went, to the ice company, the match factory, the slaughter house, and to the Kingston and Saint Andrew Bus Company, the men were ready for action, with the exception of the workers at the last stop. The busmen were slightly unsure of themselves; and what was even more surprising, they were inclined to wait and see what the new day would bring by way of a clearer and more concrete lead from Broome.

Crossman was fully prepared to meet this and deal with it, and so was Martin.

And it was Martin who spoke first; he emphasized the importance of all-round loyalty and concerted action; he told the drivers and conductors, who were there waiting to go on duty, to leave the depot and sit on the parapet of the Company fence.

Crossman took over and repeated Martin's plea, adding that there might not be another positive lead for many years to come. He spoke dramatically, in the manner of an inspired park-orator, which he knew would appeal to his listeners instinctively. He spoke for about ten minutes, and at the end of his splendid, calculated performance, the busmen, all twenty of them, walked out and sat down in front of the Company fence.

Martin detailed six men to bring in the busmen who had gone out on the early morning run, and they promised to carry out his order faithfully.

'And now for the tricky part of the operation,' Crossman said wearily, resting his hand on Martin's shoulder, as they walked away from the line of sitting men.

'Tricky?' Martin asked, chuckling quietly, nervously. 'They're "outside", which means they're already organized in a sense.'

'Organized for what, though?'

'Not for orderly action, you mean?'

'Not for what *we* want.' Crossman paused. 'A mere handful started the flare-up on the building site yesterday. We can have an explosion on our hands in next to no time.'

'Isn't that what we want? Energy and impact.'

'Our way, Martin. And our way mightn't be their way; in fact, I know it won't.'

'So, what do we do?'

'Just about to ask you.'

Martin thought about the next move. He realized that he and Crossman had to make contact with some representative section of the unemployed, and extremely quickly too. He knew that he could expect to find at least one early-morning gathering in the park at Parade or at Edelweiss Park or along Spanish Town Road, but he was not at all sure which of the three places would have just the right dynamic nucleus of a representative group.

'Any ideas?' Crossman urged. 'Time's against us.'

'We could try Spanish Town Road,' Martin suggested.

'Too far and too much of a long shot,' Crossman said.

'Might be too early for Edelweiss Park.'

'That leaves Parade.'

'Nothing to lose if we can get there in a few minutes,' Martin said hopefully.

In spite of the fact that Gerald, Shifty and Fu had tried to keep out of Miriam's way, they nevertheless met head-on with her over the matter of idling under the avocado-pear tree.

'Don't you boys have anyt'ing better to do than hangin' roun' like one-two-t'ree drop' fruit, nuh?' was her opening assault.

'Just talking,' Gerald said, trying not to sound as though he was defending Shifty, Fu and himself.

'You could find some useful work roun' the yard to do,' she said, 'like waterin' the rose-garden.'

'We're working on something private,' Gerald said.

'I can imagine,' she said sarcastically.

Shifty and Fu began moving away towards the side gate.

'You two stop where you are,' she said firmly.

They froze.

'When I was growin' up, I wasn't free an' easy like you t'ree,' she said, declaiming her last three words, with her hands describing emphatic waving motions which were meant to show her regret and her impatience all at once. 'When you grow up poor an' backward, you grow up tough as nails, an' when you grow up tough, you grow up wit' regrets.'

The boys squirmed respectfully.

'Well,' Gerald said tactfully, 'Saturday's our one day off, but we'll find something to do.'

'You've got Sunday, too,' she reminded him.

'Yes, Sunday,' he said meekly.

'Anyway, wha's this "somet'ing" you goin' to find?'

'Something useful, Miriam,' Gerald promised.

'Like readin' a book?' she asked hopefully.

'Like that, maybe.'

'An' you two?' She glared at Shifty and Fu.

Shifty nodded. Fu blinked nervously.

'We'll compare our homework,' Gerald said.

'Where?' she asked.

'At Fu's place,' he said.

Fu frowned. Shifty grinned.

Miriam snorted and said, 'I t'ink you better do the comparin' on you' own back veranda, Gerry.'

'If you like, Miriam, but you mightn't like the noise; it might be too much for you.'

'An' since when can homework make noise?'

'Comparing does.'

'Well, *compare* sof'ly.' She smiled and left them to figure out what to do.

'Let's work on our riot plan, Gerry,' Shifty suggested.

'Let's get out of Miriam's way first,' Fu said. 'Let's ride.'

'O.K.,' Gerald said. 'But we'll have to sneak off, one by one.'

'Where d'we meet?' Fu asked.

'Not far from base,' Shifty said. 'Somewhere in Cross Roads?'

'By the market?' Fu said.

'The market's good enough,' Gerald told them and snapped his fingers to mark the end of the conference.

Just at that moment, his mother appeared behind him and asked, 'Why the market, Gerry? What's going on between you and Shifty and Fu?'

Shifty stood with his mouth open and his shoulders defensively raised.

Fu grinned idiotically and hung his head.

Gerald faced his mother and said, 'We were thinking of going for a ride as far as the market. Just for a chat. Just to get out of Miriam's way.'

'You won't be in her way on the veranda, Gerry, front or back,' Jessica said, 'and what's more, you know why you mustn't go out today.'

As she walked away, her shoulders dropping and rising rhythmically like a stalking teacher well satisfied, the boys felt that their spirit of adventure had been dampened so coolly that they would certainly need time to summon enough new enthusiasm to start planning again.

Gerald pointed to the front veranda and said, 'We knew it wouldn't be easy.'

'That's exactly what I said,' Fu agreed readily. 'We won't be able to make a move, no how!'

'We'll see,' Shifty said, deflating Fu's pessimistic outcry.

'Of course, we'll see –' Gerald backed up Shifty's remark, '– and we'll make out, if we take the risks and don't panic.'

Shifty looked at Fu, and then he hopped a few paces and landed beside Gerald, and they walked towards the steps of the veranda.

Fu shrugged in the way he usually did whenever he was being left out in the cold, and for no reason, other than to baffle and irritate them both, he began to whistle:

John tu-wit
Sweet John.

8

Martin and Crossman were hurrying along East Queen Street, weaving their way through a procession of slow cyclists and a few loitering beggars and hopscotching boys and girls. The street bore no signs of tension or of the coming upheaval. It looked as it always did at that hour, shabby and half-awake.

Parade looked even shabbier and drowsier. The trucks and cars were moving slowly around the four sides of the vast square; the bicycles were making tiny zigzagging motions as their riders pedalled along irregular tracks between the middle of the street and the gutter beneath the pavement. The trees in the park were dusty and still. The dullness of their green leaves matched the dull glaze in the eyes of the men, who were huddled in the far north-west corner, and whom Martin and Crossman were approaching cautiously.

'What do we say to them?' Crossman said. 'How do we begin?'

Martin stared at the men and said to Crossman, 'Wait for them to make the first move, I suppose.'

'And if they don't?'

'They will.'

And they did. A young man, with a bandaged wrist and a badly bruised face, waved and invited them to join the group.

As Martin and Crossman were getting closer, the man grinned and said amiably, 'Missa Crossman, I see you' comin' to cash in on the 'appenin'. You, too, Missa Manson.'

Crossman threw his arms up in the air and pretended that he

was welcoming the group, rather than the other way round, and Martin smiled.

'Wha' you smilin' for, Missa Manson?' the man asked bluntly. 'You ashamed of Missa Crossman or wha'?'

'Why should I be ashamed of anybody or anything?' Martin asked, smiling broadly and imitating Crossman's expansive gesture of welcome.

'So you come to organize the down-an'-out, then?' the man said.

'What's your name?' Crossman asked.

'They call me Big Man.'

'You're the leader here?' Martin said, making his accent and his inflexion as comradely as he could manage at such short notice.

'You could call me tha', yes,' Big Man boasted affably, inverting the real deep feeling of pride he felt in his position in the group.

'Thought of anything yet?' Crossman asked him.

'We don't bother to t'ink up anyt'ing, Missa Crossman; we go out an' do.'

'Do what, Big Man?' Martin asked.

'Like wha' 'appen yesterday.'

'At the building site?' Crossman asked.

'You guess' correc', Missa Crossman.'

'Is that where you got hurt?' Martin asked.

'Same place.'

'So, what're you going to do today? Crossman asked.

'Today will take care o' itself, natural-like.'

'How *natural*?' Martin asked.

'You'll see, Missa Manson,' Big Man said, turning to the group which was silently appreciating the exchange between its 'leader' and the two 'strike officials'.

'We've been going the rounds of the docks and the factories and so on,' Martin offered, hoping that the information would make Big Man better disposed towards Crossman and himself.

'We know you' been organizin' the workin' people from early o' clock,' Big Man said, 'an', as a matter o' fac', we was wonderin' when you was goin' catch up with us in the park.'

'Do you want us to suggest anything?' Martin asked him.

'Sugges' wha' you want. Words can't do no damage. Yes, Missa Manson, talk you' talk.'

Martin looked at Crossman. It was a look of near-anguish and tense expectation.

Crossman threw back his head, opened his arms wide and told the group that he and Martin wanted to hold a mass meeting of as many of the unemployed men and women in Kingston as Big Man could gather quickly in the park within an hour. He went on, equally confidently, to say that he wanted to talk to them about the meaning of the rioting at Broome, and about their present situation in Kingston.

Big Man listened attentively, and when Crossman was finished, he asked, 'Wha' 'bout the police?'

Crossman clapped his hands with conviction, gazed around the park and said, 'We'll talk to them, too, if they come. Why not?'

'Besides, we won't be breaking the law, I don't think,' Martin added, very nearly parodying his own self-doubt. 'In any case, *words can't do no damage.*'

Big Man laughed loudly at Martin's well-timed 'back-chat'. The group registered its appreciation with an applause of guffaws and heavy sighs; the raucous laughter came mainly from the young men in the group and the slow, deep, throaty sighs of approval from the older men.

'O.K.,' Big Man promised. 'Right here in the park, Missa Crossman an' Missa Manson, in one hour from now, as you say. See you then.'

The Kingston parish church clock struck seven-thirty.

9

Gerald, Shifty and Fu had formed a triangle with their chairs on the front veranda, and were keeping their voices down as they exchanged and rejected one another's suggestions for a master plan of operation during the forthcoming crisis.

Jessica was moving about quietly behind them in the sitting-room; she was clutching a batch of exercise-books which she was correcting from time to time; she always brought back a large amount of work to do, and for her, Saturday was just another working-day.

Her movements made the boys slightly nervous. Yet they continued their discussion and kept their voices down, and Gerald divided his attention between the conference and the distant sounds behind him in the sitting-room.

And, as if to make things even more difficult for the three of them, Miriam began appearing fairly frequently in the side-yard at the corner of the veranda where the group was sitting.

'Cannon to the left,' Fu said, 'and cannon to the right.'

'Keep talking and they won't suspect anything,' Gerald ordered.

'But we've run out of ideas, Gerry,' Shifty pleaded.

'What've we decided on so far?' Gerald asked.

'Nothing much,' Fu said.

'We've got one or two things settled,' Shifty intervened.

'Like wha'?' Fu challenged him.

'Well, we've got telephones and we've got radios.'

'And,' Fu cut in, 'the telephones are all on a single party-line, which means we'll be listening in to ourselves. Big deal!'

Fu's wilful ridicule annoyed Shifty and Gerald.

'Look, Fu-*fool*!' Gerald said. 'We won't be listening in; we'll be *monitoring* the conversations we pick up and only those that're about what's happening outside in the upheaval. Secondly, our phones are not on a single party-line; we're all on separate lines from one another, even though they are party-lines, which means we'll have three different sources of information coming in.'

Fu blinked.

'And something else,' Shifty added. 'We've got the radio to listen to.'

'That!' Fu exclaimed. His lack of enthusiasm was obvious.

'And what's wrong with the news?' Gerald asked. 'We've got to listen to it.'

'More music than anything else,' Fu pointed out, 'and besides, everybody'll be listening to the radio.'

'So, why shouldn't we?' Shifty asked. He was clearly exasperated.

Jessica came out to the veranda and stood a short distance away

56

from them and smiled. 'D'you see?' she said. 'A teacher's work's never done.' She patted the exercise-books.

Shifty and Fu forced a respectful smile, and Gerald shifted uneasily.

10

Martin and Crossman had left the park and walked briskly across Parade to Crossman's cabinet-maker's shop in West Street which also served as the founding office of the C.I.T.U. headquarters. There, Crossman made what Martin thought was the most impressive gesture he had seen him make for the morning: he explained the Union plan for the day to the six men working in his shop and told them to go home and come back on Monday morning; and, before they left, he gave them an extra 'time-and-a-half' bonus payment for the loss of the working-day which he was forced to deprive them of by his Union order. The men were silently grateful and showed their gratitude by discreetly leaving a half-crown each behind on their workbenches, as their contributions to the Union dues which Crossman had been collecting on and off from those workers who were willing and able to contribute.

Crossman closed the shop, and he and Martin got into the old delivery van which was parked at the back of the building, and drove to Martin's house to work on their speeches for the emergency mass meeting.

The first person to greet them was Gerald who was sitting on the front veranda with Shifty and Fu, listening to the news-flashes on the radio. He jumped off the veranda and ran down to the gate and announced, 'They're coming into Kingston. They're almost here by now, Dad. Have you heard?'

Martin frowned and asked, 'Who're coming, Gerry?'

Gerald literally gulped down his excitement and hesitated.

Shifty and Fu leapt off the veranda, raced down the gravel path and stood on either side of him.

'Who're you talking about?' Martin asked again.

'The people from Broome, Dad. All of them.'

'All the rioters and crowds of others from the country districts around Broome,' Shifty added.

'How many of them?' Crossman asked.

'Hundreds,' Fu said.

'They've been marching and travelling in donkey-carts all night last night,' Gerald said.

'They'll be here, in town, any time now, so the radio says,' Shifty stressed.

Crossman walked up to the veranda and sat down in silence; Gerald, Shifty and Fu, with Martin in the lead, followed close behind.

Gerald watched the preoccupied stillness on the faces of his father and Crossman, and continued listening to the radio, which, at that moment, was broadcasting light classical music. Martin was sitting on the edge of his chair and holding his head on the slant, in his characteristically pensive 'tracker's position', as though he were listening to the faintest possible animal sounds on the surface of the veranda floor. Crossman was sitting well back in his chair and slowly pounding his right fist into the open palm of his left hand.

'Heard the news?' Jessica said, coming through the sitting-room door.

Martin looked up at her and nodded.

Crossman stood and paid his respects.

Gerald offered his mother his chair and drew up another for himself.

Miriam appeared soon afterwards and asked, 'Look' like trouble comin', Missa Martin?'

'Good trouble, Miriam,' Martin told her, 'if we can put it to work constructively.'

'An' you, Missa Crossman?'

'I think the same, Miriam,' Crossman said.

'You scared, Miriam?' Gerald teased her.

'Wha' is laugh to you is deat' to me,' Miriam said and changed the topic with her inevitable invitation: 'You all better eat somet'ing substantial before you do any more master plannin'. Wha' you want?'

Her use of 'master plannin'' was intended as gentle mockery, and Martin and Crossman looked at her and smiled.

'We won't always be without power, you know, Miriam,' Crossman said.

'I think she knows that,' Martin said. 'I believe she doubts that you and I will ever make it. But if we do?' Then he turned to her and asked, 'Trying to make your peace from now, eh, Miriam, if we do?'

'If a little food is makin' peace,' she said, 'then i's peace I' makin', yes.' She started walking away.

'Lemonade and extras will do, Miriam,' Jessica called after her. Then she turned to Martin and said, 'Your son's been bursting to give you the news about Broome. Has he?'

Martin nodded.

'What's going to happen?' she asked.

Before he could reply, Crossman said, 'Martin and I'll be talking to a mass meeting later on.'

'Will the Broome crowd be there by then?' she asked, her voice showing a trace of personal concern for the safety of both men.

'I hope so,' Martin said.

'Nothing could be better,' Crossman added.

During the conversation, Gerald, Shifty and Fu had made a mental note of the mass meeting and had decided on their own course of action. They wanted to know more about the meeting, but they did not want to arouse the Mansons' suspicions. They hoped that Martin and Crossman would say something more about the time and the place, before they passed on to another topic.

'Do you think there'll be any violence?' Jessica asked.

'There could be,' Martin said.

'There's bound to be, Jessica,' Crossman said. 'They're in the mood for it. To what extent, nobody knows. But coming to Kingston isn't a picnic for them. That's plain.'

'Do you want violence, Mr. Crossman?' Gerald asked.

'Not really, Gerry. At least, not violence just for the sake of violence.'

'But what, Mr. Crossman?' Fu asked.

'Well, maybe a show of protest against the existing misery and bad conditions generally for the working people all over the country.'

'Won't the police be out in force?' Shifty asked, making his question sound like a statement.

'And the army, if necessary,' Martin said.

'Martial law might be declared,' Crossman said. 'Curfew restrictions. The whole works, in fact.'

Jessica shifted in her chair. She felt uneasy and extremely worried about the events of the immediate future. Of course, she was convinced of one thing: she definitely wanted all the possible improved conditions for the workers and she wanted to see the proper establishment of the C.I.T.U. with which Martin was closely associated; but she was desperately anxious about the effect of the Broome marchers on the situation in Kingston.

A news-flash was about to be announced and Gerald duly cautioned everybody, got up, and stood by the sitting-room window nearest the radio. After a few seconds' silence, the announcer's voice came over with appropriate urgency: 'The mile-long procession of marchers from Broome, which has been on the roads since last night, is reported to be approaching the corporate area. The procession is orderly and showing signs of

60

fatigue and drowsiness. It is believed that the bulk of the marchers will be going directly to the park at Parade where Mr. Alexander Crossman, the cabinet-maker and self-styled leader of the so-called Crossman's Industrial Trades Union, is expected to address a mass meeting of unemployed men later this morning. Stand by for further news-flashes.'

Gerald, Shifty and Fu knew, now, where the meeting was going to be held; they only had to find out the time. Gerald sat down and waited to hear what either his father or Crossman was going to say about the news-flash.

'They got hold of that pretty quickly,' Crossman said. 'They've even put two and two together about the marchers and the mass meeting. I like the "It is believed…" bit.'

'We're marked men,' Martin suggested light-heartedly, but the urgency in his voice betrayed him.

'The police will be waiting,' Shifty said.

'And, if I know them, they'll be ready for the slightest sign of trouble,' Crossman confirmed. 'Ready and waiting to pounce.'

Martin nodded.

'Gosh!' Fu exclaimed, and then quickly covered his mouth with his hand. Gerald frowned at him, and Shifty sighed despairingly.

'But trouble won't really serve your purpose, will it?' Jessica asked, begging to be reassured that Martin and Crossman would do everything possible to avoid an outbreak of mob violence.

'What has to be,' Crossman told her, 'has to be, Jessica.'

Martin got up and started pacing the edge of the veranda. He stopped quite suddenly and pointed to Crossman.

Jessica looked anxiously from Martin to Crossman, and back again.

Gerald, Shifty and Fu gaped intently at both men.

Crossman frowned. 'What's wrong?' he said, a little disturbed at Martin's apparently accusing gesture.

'I've got it!' Martin said.

'What?' Crossman asked, still puzzled and upset.

'You've got to go out and meet them and lead them into the meeting,' Martin said, proud of his split-second inspiration and smiling confidently to show that he really was.

'Good idea,' Crossman said. 'But what about the others at the meeting? What about Big Man? He won't know I'm coming. He'll think I've ducked out.'

'No, he won't,' Martin said. 'I'll be at the park. I'll hold on for you.'

'Right.'

Crossman's ready faith in Martin's plan pleased Martin enormously.

'I think you should put yourself at the head of the procession and march in with it.' Martin repeated his proposal and continued: 'And I'll be all right with Big Man and the others. I'll send for Marcus. In fact, I'll call in everybody. I'll send for the foundry men, the dockers, and the rest of the strike force. Everybody!'

Crossman agreed.

Jessica felt a certain concealed pride in Martin's proposal. Gerald, too, looked proudly at his father, and, at the same time, told himself finally what he had to do about his secret thoughts concerning the mass meeting.

Miriam came out with a tray of corned beef sandwiches and pickle, and ice-cold lemonade mixed with 'coolie foot' sugar and limes. She handed Jessica the tray and said, 'Victory feas' before the victory.' She went back inside, muttering to herself.

Martin and Crossman ate quickly, rehearsed the order of the essential talking-points in their speeches, memorized them, and left the house.

Gerald, Shifty, Fu and Jessica stood together and waved Martin and Crossman goodbye. And before the van moved off, Miriam came out on to the veranda and stood beside Gerald. She nudged him and said, 'Wha' a lot a' fuss an' botheration jus' to get one little Union start' up. I 'ope it wort' it in the long run.'

Gerald looked at her and shrugged.

11

Crossman drove straight to the west end of Kingston and got out along Spanish Town Road. Martin then took over and drove to the park.

It was about eight twenty-five when he got there.

He saw a very large gathering spread round the two banyan trees at the north-east corner.

Big Man introduced him to the gathering and Martin stood on the highest loop of the adventitious roots of the taller banyan which provided him with a ready-made platform, and addressed the mass meeting. He explained Crossman's delay. He went on to tell the patient and trusting throng of unemployed men and women about the Union's plan to incorporate the Broome marchers into the meeting. Then he asked for a few volunteer-messengers to step forward. About a dozen eager young men came forward and Martin asked them to go out and bring in all the strike-groups which had been organized earlier. He thanked the volunteers and continued his address.

When Marcus arrived with the men from the foundry, Martin called him to his side and introduced him to the gathering. Marcus made a short speech and pledged his support of the Union.

The last set of strikers to arrive were the busmen who were followed almost immediately afterwards by two inspectors of police, a number of sergeants, and a full complement of police constables. They took up their positions in a loose cordon round the gathering, and a few actually stood near the banyan.

Unknown to Martin, Gerald, Shifty and Fu had parked their Rudges on the inside of the north-east fence and had crept in among the men standing at the back of the banyan, where, they felt certain, Martin would not be able to see them. Yet, the position of their hiding-place was such that they were able to catch glimpses of Martin in profile, particularly when he turned to emphasize a point to either side of the gathering.

Gerald looked nervously round the park every now and then, conscious of his daring disobedience and deception, and wondered when his mother and Miriam would discover that he was not at home; he had slipped out of the house ostensibly to clean the wheels of his bicycle and to tighten the nuts and wing-bolts which usually have to be looked at every day. He had made sure, in his deception, that his mother and Miriam had seen him preparing to do his daily chores on the Rudge, thus making it easy for him to be left alone so that he would be able to escape without being spotted.

Now, he was feeling strangely conscience-stricken about his behaviour, but it was too late to do anything about it: he tingled at the prospect of witnessing the actual beginning of the upheaval which his father had been talking about for such a long time. So far, the signs had not been dramatic at all; there had hardly been any 'signs' as such, just talk and more talk and nothing that promised real suspense and action. Nevertheless, the part being played by his father was enough to sustain Gerald's expectations for a while; he felt proud of his father's dominant position at the meeting, and wondered if any of the men had recognized him as his son.

He, Shifty and Fu were the only boys in the park, as far as Gerald could see, and this made him uneasy. Perhaps the police would soon notice this, perhaps not; he hoped not; but, even more than that, he would not have known what to do or what to say if his father had seen him.

A bus-driver, who was standing beside Gerald, patted his shoulder and asked, 'But, don't I know you from somewhere, sonny boy?'

Gerald looked up and struggled against an urge to run away; he was shaken by the man's question and was trying hard not to show it.

'I' sure I' seen you racin' 'gainst my bus at evenin' time when school let out,' the man insisted.

Gerald tried to ignore his questioner's insistence.

Shifty and Fu were preparing to scamper at the first sign from Gerald.

The man paused for a while and stood with his right hand supporting his chin and stared at Gerald.

'Yes,' he said, shaking his head in the convinced way of someone solving a problem of recognizing a familiar face. 'I know you' face a'right. You ride a Rudge bicycle. Right?'

Gerald nodded.

Shifty and Fu wondered why he admitted it. They virtually held their breath and waited to see what would happen next.

'You go to Kingston College?' the man asked.

Gerald nodded again.

'An' you live somewhere in Cross Roads?'

Gerald looked away and began edging his way through a tight knot of men huddled together and conveniently providing a solid phalanx behind which he could hide himself.

But the man reached out and grabbed his arm and said, 'Useless you tryin' to pop me, sonny. I figure people' face' like a pack o' poker cards. You's Missa Manson' boy. I know so. Yes?'

All that Gerald could do, at that crucial moment, was to tear himself away from the man's grasp, signal to Shifty and Fu, change direction, and push himself headlong into another thick knot of men standing at the fringe of the roots of the banyan. This brought him within a matter of a few feet from the place in which his father was standing. He took a quick look behind him to see if the man was coming after him, but he was not. Gerald breathed easily, but not for long, because, from his vantage point, his father seemed to be looking straight at him every time he lowered his head while appealing to the cluster of the gathering immediately in front of him. And again, standing nearby, there was a fruit vendor whom Gerald recognized as one of the regular Cross Roads market women and who, he was certain, would recognize him at a glance. He tried to make himself small, as was only natural for someone in his plight to imagine possible, but he soon discovered that it was, indeed, a physical impossibility. He prayed that the woman would not look his way. And of course, his squirming movements, his attempts 'to make himself small', were simply exposing him more and more to the attention of the people clustered round him.

This was the predicament he found himself in when a burst of applause sounded throughout the park, followed by volley after successive volley of ear-splitting shouting and rasping whistling. Then came the furious helter-skelter movement of the gathering towards the roadway at the centre of the park.

Gerald was thankful for the distraction and seized the opportunity to get as far away from the bus-driver and the market woman as he could manage. He looked around for Shifty and Fu, and saw them running towards their bicycles. He shouted and waved to them, and ran to the loops of the adventitious roots under the banyan and climbed up, as quickly as he could, in order to see what was going on. He got to the top before the dust of the stampeding gathering could rise high enough to blot out his view. He tipped upwards and what he saw coming towards him was the most awe-inspiring spectacle he had ever seen in his life.

Shifty and Fu joined him.

About five hundred men and women, some with bandanas, some bareheaded, and many with old, tattered straw boaters and grease-stained felt hats, and with sweating, smiling faces and tired, glassy eyes and elated, self-assured gestures, were billowing like a sea of mounting waves gradually generating the kind of energy which would inevitably deluge even the broadest existing landmass with its slow, final oceanic force.

Gerald, Shifty and Fu watched the panoramic expanse of movement getting closer and closer to them and their bodies shivered with excitement. Their faces and arms suddenly broke out in a rash of goose-pimples and they became light-headed; they felt almost transported. They struggled against the mesmeric effect of the spectacle and tipped higher and managed to reach a low branch of the banyan. They deftly swung themselves on to the back of the branch and settled down to take in the approaching magnificence of the marchers. Gerald saw his father fighting to clear a path for the narrowing front-line column, and he was able to see, for the first time, the overall shape of the newcomers. They had formed the pattern of a vast delta, spread out across the length and breadth of Parade. The back of the triangular mass was filled with cyclists walking beside their bicycles and with hand-cartmen pushing their empty carts and with other people who had attached themselves to the marchers. The apex of the delta, which was now near to the roots of the banyan, was narrow and slow-moving.

Martin had become a part of it. And so had Big Man and Marcus. And walking a few feet in front of them, with his arms outstretched and his head tilted arrogantly backwards, was the tall, impressive figure of Alexander Crossman, his Panama hat, white drill suit and white boots speckled with dust and splashes of mud and brown watermarks of sweat and stained wrinkles.

The police seemed to be everywhere. They were dotted all over the park and outside too. There must have been, all within a matter of a few minutes, several reinforcements added to the original number. There were at least four inspectors and six superintendents walking along the V of the delta, inching their way closer towards Crossman with each step they took.

Gerald decided to climb higher into the banyan when he saw that Crossman was heading directly towards the roots of the tree. Gerald told Shifty and Fu what he wanted to do, and they found a comfortable position on a branch about ten feet above the loops of the roots on which, Gerald reckoned, Crossman would stand; and huddled together, they sat still and waited to see what was going to happen. They began watching the police intently. They wondered about the look on their faces.

As far as they could make out, the police looked collectively anxious, as if they were on the verge of some kind of anticipated offensive action.

Crossman mounted the highest loop of roots and spread his arms wide, and, without actually calling for silence, managed to get it by merely looking round him and waving the palms of his hands in a series of gentle, downward, flapping motions. An incredible wave of silence swept over the park; even the roar of the traffic in Parade seemed to subside to a distant rumble.

Crossman relaxed his demagogic pose, and the attitude he assumed was one of cool dignity and compassion; he looked like the popular leader he had been striving to become over the years; he was the man whom the people could trust. The hundreds of people below him were standing absolutely still, looking upwards and waiting to hear what their new leader was about to say to them.

Gerald looked around for his father. He saw him standing on the ground on the right of Crossman. Marcus and Big Man were also on the ground on Crossman's left.

Suddenly there was an angry upsurge of voices from the front of the crowd, and Gerald, Shifty and Fu leant over the branch to see what had caused it, They were just in time to glimpse the leaping figures of two police constables as they sprang and landed on the loop of roots on which Crossman was standing.

'Tarzan and Jane,' Fu whispered.

Shifty suppressed a raucous laugh and uttered a couple of muffled gulps.

'Me, Fu,' Fu said.

'Shut up!' Gerald said hoarsely.

Fu grinned and beat a soft tattoo on his breast and settled down again.

In the meantime, the two constables had taken up their positions on either side of Crossman and had planted their feet securely apart and folded their arms. Each rested his elbow on the handle of his baton which was lying in the slit along his side pocket.

Crossman restored order effortlessly, smiled at the constables and began almost chattily, 'I must be a very important man to be given this sort of preferential treatment from the police, which reminds me that some of it, some of this *same* consideration, is long overdue to all of us gathered here this morning.'

There was a crackling shower of hand-clapping and exclamations of agreement.

Fu leant against Shifty and said, 'Ol' Crossman is another word-merchant.'

Shifty nodded.

'Our meeting today is all about *that*!' Crossman began again. 'It's manifestly about the new deal that's supposed to be ours, that we're demanding, that we must get from our Government and from our employers.' He paused.

He had planned to begin his speech by not 'talking down' to his listeners. He knew that they demanded a level of sparkle from the man they would choose to follow, but he also knew that he would not be expected to keep it up throughout. He had to get back gradually to the language and the lush, hearty expressiveness of the 'grass roots' leader; a bright, high-flown beginning was essential, and an earthy, popular appeal was absolutely necessary for the rest of his speech.

'We're not cattle!' he boomed. 'We're not slaves or beasts of the field, or dumb, driven oxen, or fools; we are flesh and blood; we are people with human emotions, pride, and feelings that can get hurt, indeed, that have been hurt, time and time again.'

A *whoop* of appreciative sighs oozed round the park.

Crossman clasped his hands and nodded graciously.

Fu saluted the gathering and then turned quickly to see if Gerald had been watching him. Gerald had. All he did was to frown at Fu and gaze down again at Crossman.

'We are people with dreams! With ambitions. With hopes and a future to plan for, whatever the Government may think to the contrary, and whatever our employers, in all their glory, may think they have the right to think.'

One of the Broome marchers, a tall, thin woman, with a haggard face and large, wild eyes, made a megaphone with her hands in front of her mouth and groaned loudly, 'Lawd, 'ave mercy!'

Again, Crossman clasped his hands and nodded.

'More than all these things, we are workers! We are labourers, factory hands, apprentices, cane-cutters, tallymen, bus-drivers, conductors, dockers, foundry-men, street-traders, market-people, *workers all*, with nothing coming to us, nothing to protect us, and with nothing in view except wicked exploitation, starvation wages and no voice to speak up for us. No collective voice. But worse than that!'

The woman from Broome, again, called out, 'Bad! Real, real bad!'

And Crossman continued: 'Yes, much worse than that: most of us are unemployed, out of work, down and out, poverty-stricken, shunned, scorned, abused, forgotten!'

At that point, there was a concerted exclamation of 'True word!' 'Less than dirt!' 'That's so!' 'Yes!'

Crossman smiled.

The two constables looked unconcerned but still officially on guard, rigid and watchful.

Gerald muttered, 'Great, eh?'

Shifty said, 'Fantastic.'

Fu said, 'Wait for the grab, man.'

'What grab?' Gerald asked.

'You wait and see,' Fu said. 'Boun' to come.'

Crossman went on, 'We need representation. We should've had it long ago. We want it *now*.'

There was a roar of affirmation.

Two inspectors of police, who were standing a few inches away from the loop, drew closer to each other, and one whispered something to the other and pointed to Crossman; the other inspector nodded and moved away.

Gerald, Shifty and Fu noticed this and kept a close watch on the inspector's movement. They saw him inching his way up to the foot of the loop, and when he got there, he signalled one of the constables flanking Crossman to get down and come to him. The constable did so quickly, stood at attention and listened to the inspector's instructions. Then the constable climbed back on to the loop and stood at ease.

But Gerald, Shifty and Fu had been watching him; they saw him wink at the other constable, make a sly 'palms-up' sign to him and look away innocently.

'See what I mean?' Fu whispered urgently.

'What?' Gerald asked, keeping his voice well down to a mutter.

'The grab's going to be a "push".'

'Is that what the signal meant?' Shifty asked.

'Just that,' Fu said. 'You watch.'

Gerald was disturbed. He wanted to warn Crossman. He felt confused, helpless, depressed.

Crossman was saying, 'I am offering myself as your representative. I am saying to you, my Brothers and Sisters, that I pledge myself, my years of experience as a working man, my energy and good faith, my honesty of purpose and my life – I pledge my Union. *Your* Union!'

Another roar of affirmation, together with a burst of deafening applause.

The two constables shifted their positions slightly, and one looked up into the banyan. As he did so, his eyes met and made four with Gerald's. The constable gazed at Shifty, then at Fu, and back again at Gerald. Gerald did not attempt to look away, but instead, he stared down at the constable and was prepared to outstare him. But the constable risked a small patronizing smile, lowered his head and continued to stare blankly, officially, over the gathering in the park.

Gerald felt quietly victorious about the incident. He knew that the constable could not really object to his being in the banyan, and besides, he was aware that the constable was under orders to stand guard by Crossman, but the patronizing smile annoyed Gerald. Anyway he soon forgot the matter, because Crossman was, by then, launching an attack on the rot in the society, as he saw it: 'We don't respect ourselves as a people. We don't even know who we are. We have been kept from getting to know our destiny and our path towards it. We've been fooled. We've been blinded. We haven't had a chance to realize our true worth as human beings. This is wrong! It's criminal! It has to stop. Workers, unite! Unite now in the Union. *Our* Union will protect us!'

One of the Broome marchers pushed his way up to the front and shouted, 'We will follow you, Missa Crossman! We will follow you 'til we die!'

The crowd, behind him, took up the rallying cry and repeated it over and over again, until it became a lilting refrain:

'We – will fol–low Miss–a Cross–man
We – will fol–low Miss–a Cross–man
We – will fol–low Miss–a Cross–man
We – will fol–low Miss–a Cross–man
'til – we – die!'

The refrain was quickly strengthened by a rhythmic tattoo of stamping feet, and soon afterwards, that was followed by a barrage of loud hand-clapping. After a while, the whole gathering began to surge forward, aiming its enormous energy at the roots of the banyan.

The police went into action immediately. They drew their batons and threatened to beat back the front line. But to no avail.

It was then that the signal was given from the ground, and Crossman was pushed off the loop and held below by the two inspectors.

It was all done so quickly and so neatly that very few of the people in the front line saw it. But Gerald, Shifty and Fu did, from above.

And so did Martin and Marcus and Big Man. But they could do nothing to intervene, because of the swirl and flurry of movement and confusion everywhere around them. However, they fought their way clear of the excited crowd and caught up with the police who were holding on to Crossman and leading him towards the back door of a Black Maria which was parked near the north-east corner of the park.

Martin ran to the side of the Black Maria and spoke to one of the inspectors. 'Why're you taking him away?' he asked breathlessly, imploring and yet showing a trace of anger in his voice.

'Isn't it obvious?' the inspector said.

'No, it isn't,' Martin objected.

'Let's say we're giving him the protection he needs,' the inspector said.

'Does that mean that you're arresting him?'

'What do you think?'

'Well, *are* you?'

The inspector turned away abruptly, shrugging off Martin's question.

Martin then went round to the back of the Black Maria to see if he could speak to Crossman before he was taken away, but he had already been locked inside.

As the Black Maria moved off, the milling crowd in the park began to sing:

'We – will – fol–low Miss–a Cross–man
We – will – fol–low Miss–a Cross–man'

The police constables, who had been left on duty, were trying to get the crowd to disperse. In their over-emphatic efforts, they apparently pushed and jostled too hard and were seen to be bullying certain sections instead of dealing with the situation firmly and fairly, and this was sufficient provocation, along with the fast spreading news of Crossman's arrest, to cause the beginning of the upheaval.

The Broome marchers were the first to set the riot in motion. They fought the police viciously. They deliberately trampled the garden-beds and rockeries in their path, and when they were driven out of the park by police retaliation, they swarmed through Parade erratically, overturning parked cars, smashing shop windows and attacking cyclists and motorists in the streets.

It was not long after that that the Kingston men joined in; they began moving along North Parade and heading towards Lower Saint Andrew.

In the meantime, Gerald, Shifty and Fu had slipped out of the banyan, grabbed their bicycles, looked around for Martin, failed to find him, and had set off for home. The sudden violence had shaken them.

Martin, Marcus and Big Man had decided to go to the Central Police Station on East Queen Street to find out if they would be allowed to see Crossman and to arrange bail for him. They had driven off in his delivery van, taking the route away from the rioters' path and driving fast enough, they hoped, to catch up with the Black Maria. As they sped along the comparatively empty streets, they could hear the clamour of the rioting behind them. The shouting was angry and piercing, and the sounds of breaking glass and metallic crashes came rocketing and whistling through the air.

The time was approximately ten minutes past nine.

PART TWO

THE UPHEAVAL

CHAPTER FOUR

1

Gerald, Shifty and Fu were pedalling frantically through the side-streets and lanes off Upper King Street and pushing their Rudges to their limit over the jagged gaps, sand-traps and gravel tracery of the patchy macadam surface. They had never had to ride so emotionally before, so deliberately recklessly. The tyres of the Rudges crunched down on a number of small objects in their path, pulverizing them, while absorbing several severe skidding jolts; but still Gerald, Shifty and Fu rode their bicycles mercilessly, biting into the distance that lay between their front wheels and their destination. Their legs kept forcing the pace and firing away like long thin pistons, as their arms guided the handlebars and front forks through a massing pressure of swerves and jerks and jockeying thrusts.

As they tore along, they could not help thinking of the shambles they had left behind them in the park and at Parade, the brutal assaults and counter-assaults, the whisking-away of Crossman by the police, and the disappearance of Martin and Marcus. They thought of going back to look for Martin, but they remembered that their parents were alone at home and that, in any case, they had very little time left to sneak back into their houses; that is, if their absence had not already been discovered.

Just as they were about to enter into West Race Course, Fu looked sharply to his left and shouted, 'Bag-'n'-Pan's behind us. Somebody's chasing him.'

Gerald and Shifty turned in time to see one man, then three others, running towards Bag-'n'-Pan.

'They're ganging up on him,' Gerald said. 'Let's go see.'

'O.K.,' Shifty agreed.

'Quick,' Fu urged.

'Right!' Gerald ordered. 'Let's go.'

They braked fairly quickly and turned round in the middle of the street. But, by that time, the small mob of men had caught up with Bag-'n'-Pan and surrounded him and had begun to pelt him with green mangoes and chipped stones which were scattered all over the pavement.

As soon as the men saw Gerald, Shifty and Fu heading their way, they started to throw some of the stones at them. Fu cleverly thought of the right subterfuge to use, and so he swerved away from Gerald and Shifty, turned his face deliberately from the men and called out, 'Police comin'! A whole van-load!'

The men stopped their attack, and panic began showing in their faces as they fumbled among themselves on the pavement. One of them knocked down Bag-'n'-Pan, and right afterwards, signalled the other three to escape.

Bag-'n'-Pan was left lying on his back, his feet dangling in the gutter, and the top half of his body sprawled across the cracked pavement.

Gerald, Shifty and Fu parked their bicycles, ran up to the old

man, lifted him gently and propped him up against a wooden gate nearby. Gerald leant over him and raised his head and cradled it in his hands. Bag-'n'-Pan's head was bleeding.

'Quick!' a woman's voice called from behind the gate. 'Bring 'im this way.'

Gerald held his shoulders; Shifty his middle; and Fu his legs; and together, they lifted the old man through the gate and into the entrance of a vast tenement yard. Bag-'n'-Pan's body was frail and foul-smelling. The blood had already become clotted in the matted strands of his hair, and his face was bruised and streaked with dirt and perspiration.

The woman appeared and said, 'He live' in the back, in the las' out-room. Take 'im an' lay 'im down. I' get 'elp an' come back in a little while.'

Bag-'n'-Pan's room was small, unventilated and dusty. In every detail, it reflected his abject poverty, loneliness and sadness. On his camp-cot, there was a very thick layer of crushed, discoloured newspapers, and at the head of the cot, there was an old lumpy pillow without a slip-over. A mud-stained rocking-chair stood beside the cot, and, next to it, was a low, rectangular cargo-crate on which there were an open Bible, a jam jar with a spray of wilted ram-goat roses, and three sparkling bronze military medals.

'Gosh!' Fu said, looking round the room. 'Poor Bag-'n'-Pan.'

'Tough, eh?' Shifty said.

'Hope he's all right,' Gerald said, leaning over him and listening to his very faint breathing.

The woman returned with two other women who were carrying a basin of water, some strips of rough-torn calico bandages, a spoonful of brown sugar and an enamel mug.

The woman carrying the mug said, 'Goin' mix some sweet sugar-'n'-water an' give 'im to drink. That'll 'elp bring 'im roun'.'

'Is he going to die?' Gerald asked her.

She looked at Bag-'n'-Pan, from his head to his feet, felt his pulse, lifted the lid of his right eye, put her ear over his heart, patted his face gently, looked him up and down again, and said, 'Poor people like we an' Bag-'n'-Pan get use to dyin' a little bit every day, sonny boy.'

'Yes, but is he going to die from the beating he just got?' Gerald asked.

'We live tough,' she said.

'But what about him?' Fu asked impatiently, pointing to Bag-'n'-Pan.

'Not to worry you'self,' she said. 'Not'ing that a little res' can't cure.'

Gerald, Shifty and Fu smiled discreetly.

The women thanked them, and the one who had first called out to them at the gate said, 'You can leave 'im wit' us now. We'll take care o' 'im. An' mind 'ow you ride. Trouble brewin'.'

They left the room and ran to the gate. Before they mounted their bicycles, they looked up and down the street to make sure that the mob was not waiting around to jump out at them. When they were satisfied that the street was clear, they sprinted away after a long run-and-jump start.

They pedalled even harder when they got to the foot of the incline on Slipe Road, and the Rudges responded like thoroughbreds at their peak. Just as they were passing the halfway point between Torrington Bridge and Cross Roads, they heard some yelping noises, followed by a scream and a resounding crash, and they saw a woman running up the road in front of them, with another mob of men, chasing and taunting her. Then, they saw a gaping hole in the windscreen of a parked car, through which they glimpsed the driver's face, which was resting sideways on the steering-wheel, with blood streaming down his cheek. Gerald quickly sized up the situation: he reckoned that the woman must have been sitting beside the driver and had run away after the men had made their attack. He realized what he had to do to help her, so he said to Shifty and Fu, 'I'll try to get her.' And he pedalled with extra effort, caught up with her, hooked his left forearm round her waist, swept her on to the crossbar of the Rudge and took off again without losing much of his top speed; fortunately, she was light enough for him to have been able to snatch her up in one clean sweep and slip her neatly into place. She was so surprised at what Gerald had done that she sat quite motionless and rested her head and the right side of her body along the length of his right arm.

Shifty and Fu were riding purposely behind Gerald and looking around to see if they were being followed, and at the same time, covering him on either side.

After riding furiously for about five hundred yards, Gerald put the woman down at Cross Roads, and after thanking him, she ran towards the police station; and then he eased up on his pedalling and cruised the remaining three hundred yards or so of the way, straight up to the side gate of his house. Shifty and Fu came alongside and dismounted.

They looked at one another, and made no comment.

Everything was quiet.

They parted for the time being and went to their homes.

Gerald's nerves were tingling. The tension throughout his body was gradually subsiding, and his limbs were losing their stiffness, as his muscles twitched with shooting pains and spasmodic numbness.

He tiptoed into the sitting-room, switched on the radio, turned the volume down low, and waited to hear the latest news. Try as he did to suppress his heavy breathing, it continued to rise and sink and boom.

His mother was resting in her bedroom, and Miriam was ironing in her room at the back of the kitchen.

Martin, Marcus and Big Man had arrived at the Central Police Station on East Queen Street. They had been shown into the duty officer's room and had made several attempts to secure Crossman's bail; first, with requests to the inspector of police who had made the arrest, then, to his second-in-command, and finally, to the desk-sergeant. Martin kept on making his requests, and so did Marcus and Big Man, but they were told by each official in turn that it was not in the public's interest, or indeed in Crossman's, to release him so soon after the start of the rioting.

Very near to exasperation, Martin sighed impatiently and asked the desk-sergeant, 'May we know what you've charged the prisoner with?'

The overweight sergeant was puffed up with his own self-esteem; although he was grossly theatrical, and far from being overworked, he gave the impression of someone hard-pressed and busy. He rubbed his enormous stomach and said, 'We 'aven't charged 'im yet, you know. Wha' make' you t'ink he' been charged wit' anyt'ing?'

'You're holding him,' Martin said.

'For 'im own good an' for everybody else'.'

'For how long?'

'Until t'ings blow over. Maybe.'

'*Maybe*?'

'Maybe.'

And that was that. Martin sat down again, and Marcus and Big Man huddled close up to him.

'They goin' get 'im for incitin', I bet you,' Big Man whispered.

'Incitin' to riot is a serious charge, man,' Marcus agreed, also whispering and ducking out of the sergeant's view so that he would not be able to see him speaking or overhear what he was saying.

'He knows what we're talking about, Marcus,' Martin said. 'You might as well stand up and shout it out loud.' He seemed very depressed.

'How you t'ink t'ings goin' outside in the streets?' Big Man asked.

'From the noise we've been hearing, it must be hell an' all,' Martin said.

During the short period of time in which they had been at the station, there had been many distant bursts of angry shouting and other indistinct riot-noises echoing throughout the west end of Kingston. Together with these, there had also been the incessant coming and going of the police transport in the station yard. Martin, Marcus and Big Man counted them.

The sergeant looked their way and frowned. Then he swung himself round in his ancient swivel chair and pretended to be engrossed in the duty book in front of him.

After a very short time, he became restless with his idle pretence. He got up noisily and went to the open window facing his desk. He looked out and inhaled and exhaled vigorously, snorting and patting his stomach and *flip-flopping* his broad elastic braces. Then he strutted back to his desk and began his pretence with the duty book all over again.

The voices under the window came to his attention rather slowly, indistinctly at first, and then, with a sudden clarity: 'Let go the Chief! Let 'im go, Babylon!'

The sergeant sprang from his chair, ran to the window and shouted, 'You lucky if you see 'im for Chris'mas. Move on now!'

And the voices shouted back, half declaiming and half chanting:

> *'We – will fol–low Miss–a Cross–man*
> *We – will fol–low Miss–a Cross–man*
> *'til – we – die!'*

The sergeant slammed the window shut, bolted it, and glared at Martin, Marcus and Big Man.

Marcus bowed mock-graciously and smiled.

Big Man grinned grotesquely.

And Martin merely stared back at him coldly.

3

The rioting had spread downwards from the park at Parade, throughout lower western Kingston and mainly along the streets in the commercial sections. The obvious riot-targets had been the broad glass-frontages of the merchants'-stores and the big business houses, and the ground-floor windows and doors of the civil service offices and the other public buildings.

The rioters' sporadic and indiscriminate acts of violence and arson had brought out, in full force, the Kingston fire-brigade and the police transport services. Fire-engines were screaming through the streets, and patrol cars and Black Marias were klaxoning urgently everywhere.

But the rioting had also spread above the park, towards Upper Kingston, and beyond, into Lower Saint Andrew. And the fire-brigade and the police transport were also very much in evidence there.

Often, when the police arrived at a certain trouble-spot, all they saw was the terrible aftermath of the attack; the rioters had usually left the scene. They moved uncannily quickly, doing their destructive work like marauding ghosts.

A group of five men and two women, the very same voices who had shouted and jeered at the desk-sergeant under his window, had just left the shattered shop-front of a Chinese grocery, and was moving stealthily in Indian file along North Street; when the group got to the Government Medical Office, the leader pointed to the squat concrete building and said, 'This one!' Still moving in Indian file, the group crossed over North Street and crept through the drive-gate at the back of the office, and made a lightning search around the yard-area for any available missiles. After the required stones and tin cans and bottles and other sizeable assorted oddments from the dustbins had been collected, the group met in a tight huddle, and the leader said decisively, 'Roun' the front an' don't waste time. Jus' t'row an' run up Slipen Road towards Calabar College way.' He hunched his shoulders and led his attackers to their objective.

The two women dropped back slightly and took up 'lookout' positions on the pavement, while the five men ran up to the high wooden front door and broke it down in one dynamic assault; and, as soon as the door crashed open, they hurled a shower of stones and bottles into the reception hall, and backed away. The women then ran up to the gaping doorway and threw two small cardboard boxes of wood-shavings and litter over the thick sisal welcome-mat inside the door, and they, too, backed away smartly.

The leader looked around swiftly, flung a lighted match on to the mat, and signalled the group up Slipen Road.

4

Gerald was very restless. He wanted to see Shifty and Fu. He also wanted to know what was going on in the streets. He wanted to wake his mother. He wanted to find out about his father. He even wanted to consult Miriam about the catastrophic turn of events. The radio news-flashes were short and peculiarly uninformative;

he wondered about this for some time. Then he suddenly realized that neither his mother nor Miriam knew that the riot had begun.

Cross Roads had been unaffected so far. There had been no signs, apart from the incident with the motorist and the woman and the mob of men which he had witnessed on his way up Slipe Road. And, of course, there had been Bag-'n'-Pan. But that had been fairly far away from Cross Roads.

He could not, he reasoned guiltily, attempt to tell his mother and Miriam about the dramatic scenes in the park; his deception would be out. But he decided that he could tell them about the rioting in Kingston, based on the news-flashes which he had been listening to. He convinced himself that it *was* his duty to do so. His mother and Miriam were entitled to know that much, and after all, his father *was* involved.

He went to his mother's room and pushed the door gently, but he checked himself and thought of informing Miriam first; perhaps, she would be able to give his mother the news and save him the embarrassment of his petty deception which was weighing on his conscience. This he did, and Miriam went straight to Jessica's room and relayed the information.

The three of them met on the back veranda.

'So Crossman's been arrested, Gerry?' Jessica asked.

'According to the radio,' Gerald told her.

'Anything about your father?'

'No.'

'Marcus?'

'No.'

'I suppose it' comin' up to Cross Roads?' Miriam asked.

'Maybe,' Gerald said. 'Maybe it's here already.'

'We would've heard something,' Jessica said. 'You heard or seen anything yet?'

'No,' he lied halfheartedly, hanging his head and deliberately smoothing down his slightly tousled 'overland' hairstyle which was always a sure sign of his unease.

Jessica noticed this but she did not comment. So did Miriam.

He began feeling sorry for himself, trapped in his own deception and not being able to summon enough courage to free himself by telling the truth about his trip to the park. But even in his concealed guilt, he felt a nagging compulsion to come right out and tell his mother what he had done.

It was then that he remembered what Crossman had said to him at the foundry gate: '*Look after your mother... You can never tell...*'

'You got the radio goin'?' Miriam asked.

'Yes,' he said, raising his head slowly. 'But it's not time for another flash yet, I don't think. I've got it turned down low.'

'I wonder where your father's got to, Gerry?' Jessica asked.

'Don't know, Mama, but he must be all right. Not arrested or anything. We would've heard. Marcus would've come to tell us.'

Jessica nodded absent-mindedly. She looked extremely doubtful and worried.

'Marcus might be in gaol, too, for all we know,' Miriam suggested, 'like Missa Crossman.'

Gerald fidgeted. He told himself that Miriam's suggestion might very well prove to be really the case, which would mean that his father might also have been arrested, or he might have been seriously injured and lying in hospital somewhere.

'Sure you haven't heard anything outside?' Jessica asked him again.

'No. I haven't.'

Jessica went back to her bedroom, and Miriam shuffled off to the kitchen.

Gerald was still tense and full of remorse, but he was glad to be able to get away and make contact with Shifty and Fu.

They met under the pear tree.

'What about Miriam?' Shifty asked, calmly playing the detective and beating Fu to the question that he would naturally have asked.

'Inside,' Gerald said, winking at Fu.

'We're safer up in the tree than under it,' Fu said, ignoring Shifty's manoeuvre, and Gerald's affectionate, patronizing wink.

'Great!' Gerald said, taking Fu's suggestion seriously. 'We might see something from up there.'

'Not the pear tree,' Fu said. 'Not tall enough.'

'What about the Bombay mango tree?' Shifty asked.

'The big one out front?' Fu said, making the information more of a statement than a question.

'Done,' Gerald said, and they rushed off and climbed straight up to the highest branch, which gave them a panoramic view of Cross Roads.

5

At that very moment, an ice company wagon, packed with rioters, drove into Cross Roads and stopped outside the market.

Gerald, Shifty and Fu were watching excitedly from their tree-top 'lookout'.

The men were very quiet. They leapt from the driver's cabin and from the open storage-carriage at the back, and slipped through the main gate; they were almost on tiptoe. They ran past the market women and the stall attendants and headed straight for the superintendent's office in the centre of the market shed.

As the men burst through the door, Gerald, Shifty and Fu lost sight of them.

The men roughed up the superintendent and flung him outside, and then they started to demolish his small office. It took them about a minute to reduce it to a tangle of splintered wood and ripped ledgers and broken furniture and overturned ashtrays and waste paper.

The last man out turned quickly and broke the panes in the three small windows at the back of the office.

'There they are again,' Fu said. 'Like mad red ants!'

'Fantastic!' Shifty said.

'They mean business all right,' Gerald said, rubbing his hands expectantly.

And yet they were all three apprehensive.

The noise had thrown the whole market into panic. The floor-vendors and stallholders were stampeding out of the market gates at the side and front entrances. They had all abandoned their wares and their personal belongings and were screaming and shouting their way out to Cross Roads. Following close behind them, the rioters kicked over the displays and stands and show

baskets wherever they ran into them. A few men scooped up handfuls of fruits and vegetables and stuffed them into their pockets and into the front of their shirts, and others pelted the retreating market-people with eggs and mangoes and yams and lengths of sugar-cane.

Cross Roads rang out with the terrified screams and angry protests of the vendors and the market-officers, and with the vicious jeers and threats of the rioters. The pandemonium soon spread around the vicinity, and shopkeepers started closing their shutters and pedestrians began scampering off the streets and running for shelter into the remaining open doors in the shopping centre; and, of course, passing cyclists and motorists sped through the riot-area without stopping.

A second wagon of rioters drew up outside the market, but the men did not get out.

Gerald, Shifty and Fu strained forward to see if they could recognize them.

'Some of them were in the park,' Fu said, tapping his forehead and narrowing his eyes thoughtfully.

'They could've been, I suppose,' Shifty said.

'They were,' Gerald declared. 'They're some of the Broome marchers. Most of them are.'

'What makes you so sure, Gerry?' Shifty asked.

'The hats they're wearing,' Gerald said confidently. 'Most of the Broome men were wearing old Jippa Jappa straws.'

The driver shouted something to the other set of rioters. His order was promptly obeyed, and both wagons set off up Half Way Tree Road, towards the residential sections and garden suburbs of Upper Saint Andrew. The second wagon was filled with large mounds of rubble and stones and short sticks and lengths of iron piping.

As the wagons were passing Gerald's house, Jessica and Miriam ran out to the front veranda.

Gerald, Shifty and Fu swung down rapidly out of the tree and joined them.

Miriam eyed them suspiciously, glared at Gerald because she felt she had the right to, sighed despairingly, and said, 'They come now. I's Cross Roads' time to get it, good an' proper.'

'Let's go back inside,' Jessica said. Her hands were shaking, and her voice, although low-pitched and precise, quavered slightly.

When they were all seated round the table on the back veranda, she asked, 'Is the front locked up, Gerry?'

'Doors and windows,' he assured her. 'The last one locked was the side door we just came through.'

'And the front veranda chairs?'

'Still there, Mama.' He sensed her restrained anxiety, and felt genuinely concerned about it.

Without waiting for her to say anything else, he, Shifty and Fu ran round the side yard and brought the eight Berbice chairs back to the kitchen porch.

They moved quickly and expertly, and Miriam smiled and showed her general approval.

After they had sat down again, she folded her arms and sighed, 'Well!'

Gerald looked at her and waited.

'Where you t'ink they goin' now, eh?' she asked.

'Higher up Saint Andrew,' Fu said.

'Looks that way,' Gerald agreed.

A police station-wagon shot past with its siren going full-blast, and behind it a roaring posse of motorcycle outriders. The urgency of the sounds shattered the calm on the back veranda, and Gerald, Shifty and Fu darted sudden knowing glances at one another, stood up and started walking towards the sitting-room.

'Wha' 'bout the Rudge, Gerald?' Miriam asked.

'Round the side, Miriam. Why?'

'Jus' askin'. That's all.'

He thought twice about her question: did she see me coming in? Is she stalling because she really knows I've been out?

'Where you t'ree goin' to now then?' she asked.

'To look outside, through the window at the front,' Gerald told her, and waited to be formally released.

'Shouldn't you put the Rudge away?' Jessica said.

He didn't reply. He signalled Shifty and Fu to wait for him in the sitting-room, then he turned back, walked round the veranda to the side-yard, led his bicycle into the out-room, locked it away, and went back to Jessica and Miriam.

They both wondered about his promptness and his extreme co-operative manner; they were impressed but not altogether taken in.

Another procession of police vehicles passed by. This time, it was followed by a clanging fire-engine.

'Hell let loose somewhere,' Miriam said.

Jessica and Gerald said nothing.

'Shall I tell them now?' Gerald thought. 'Might as well. It won't be easy.'

He hesitated.

'Got to tell them about the park and about Bag-'n'-Pan and the woman on Slipe Road,' he told himself.

Jessica got up and said, 'I'll be in my bedroom if anybody wants me.'

Gerald thought about the word 'anybody'.

'Who else but Miriam and me?' he asked himself. 'Or possibly Shifty and Fu?'

Then he remembered that Marcus might call: maybe she's expecting him, maybe someone else, maybe the police with news about Dad, maybe…?

Shifty and Fu both whistled *John tu-wit*, and at the same moment, Gerald also heard the announcer's voice, and he ran into the sitting-room. Jessica and Miriam followed.

They got there in time to hear the announcer saying: '…and the outbreaks of fire are being put out as fast as they appear. The firemen and the police are working all-out to cope with the situation. The British Army regiment at Up Park Camp and the local members of the Infantry Volunteer Reserve have been called out and are assisting the police in trying to restore order.

'For listeners who have just tuned in, I repeat: a state of Island-wide emergency now exists. A curfew has been imposed. Group-meetings, however small, will not be permitted, and all members

95

of the public must be off the streets after four o'clock this afternoon.

'The time is now eleven o'clock.'

Miriam left the room and went out to the kitchen.

Gerald turned off the radio, and he, Shifty and Fu sat back in their chairs, while Gerald steeled himself to confess his guilt. Oddly enough, the news had helped.

Jessica noticed his tense attitude and asked, 'Your father ought to have come in by now, don't you think?' She was thinking of the emergency, and of the forthcoming curfew. She was trembling inwardly but trying not to show it.

Gerald did not know what to say to her. He nodded and felt the tip of his nose. He goaded his waning courage and self-respect; he had to do it now, at that very moment. He felt a lump rise up from the pit of his stomach, up to his chest, and into his throat. His mouth was dry. He swallowed hard and opened his mouth to speak. Then he looked at Shifty and Fu, and his jaws clamped shut.

Just then, there was a loud, brisk knock at the front door.

Nobody moved.

Fu frowned inquisitively. Shifty opened his mouth and placed his right thumb on his lower lip. Gerald stared at the door. Jessica held her head down and listened.

In the meantime, Miriam had come running into the room.

There was a second loud knock lower down the centre panel of the door.

Miriam moved forward and drew back when the third and fourth knocks resounded round the room.

Gerald waved her towards the radio and crept up to the door himself. Jessica waved him back, but he continued. Shifty and Fu tiptoed behind him. He held on to the key and the doorknob and was about to open the door when Jessica whispered, 'Ask who's there, first, Gerry.'

Again Gerald's throat was dry, drier than before. It seemed seconds on end before he was able to ask, 'Who's there?'

There was no answer.

He repeated his question; this time louder and confidently.

Still no answer.

Shifty tried, too. And so did Fu.

But, still no answer.

Gerald then opened the door. No one was there. He locked it and looked at his mother.

'Strange,' she said.

'Funny, yes,' Miriam added.

'Might've been someone from Dad,' Gerald suggested.

'Didn't wait long,' Jessica said. 'I wonder why?'

'Don't think it could've been anyone else,' he told her.

'Like one o' the rioters?' Miriam asked.

Shifty looked at Fu, and then they both looked at Gerald.

Gerald did not reply. He suddenly remembered what he had been about to do when the knocking had interrupted him, and he sat on the chair beside the radio and said, 'I've got something to tell you, Mama.'

'What is it, son?' Her voice betrayed her mounting anxiety. She turned round and looked at him, her eyes staring with alarm and with the anticipation of overwhelming sadness.

He glanced at her sheepishly and felt his courage draining away, leaving him indecisive. He knew that he had waited too long. Besides, he had chosen the wrong time. He was acutely aware of his awkward handling of the situation and wished that he had never attempted to do anything about it. And there was the added humiliation of confessing in front of Shifty and Fu.

'What're they going to think of me?' he wondered. 'They might even spread awkward rumours among the boys at school. Perhaps they would prefer if I said nothing at all.'

He looked directly at his mother, and as he stared into her eyes, he imagined that she was expecting him to report something extremely heart-rending: the death of his father perhaps, or the destruction of the Kingston Foundry by fire, or something equally terrible.

Jessica waited for a few seconds, and when he made no attempt to reply to her question, she asked, 'Is it about your father, Gerry?'

'No,' he said timidly, 'not about Dad. It's about me. It's about what I did early this morning and again not so long ago.'

Shifty and Fu were startled and were trying not to show their concern. Gerald avoided looking their way.

'What did you do, Gerry?' Jessica asked.

He was about to speak when he, Jessica, Miriam, Shifty and Fu heard a rapid succession of clumping sounds outside. They listened carefully, straining every nerve and tilting their bodies slightly forwards.

They quickly recognized that the sounds were rather heavy footsteps on the front veranda. They were moving along the length of the outer part, next to the potted plants, and stopping and starting intermittently.

Soon afterwards, the knocking at the front door began again.

Gerald got up. So did Shifty and Fu. Jessica whispered, 'Remember, ask who's there.'

Gerald went up to the door and said quite firmly, his voice composed and confident, 'Who's that?'

There was no reply.

'Who's out there?' Gerald asked again.

Still no reply.

Shifty and Fu drew closer to Gerald and clenched their fists. Gerald took out the key and bent to the keyhole. He saw the lower half of a pair of khaki trousers; the person was standing right up against the door.

Gerald stared at the trousers and slowly he tried to recall where he had last seen that particular pair. There was a large oval grease-stain on the left leg and an even larger one on the right leg. He withdrew and smiled at Shifty and Fu, as he said, 'I know who it is. It's all right.'

Jessica looked relieved.

Miriam, however, was still noticeably apprehensive.

'You' better make sure, Gerry. Don't open up yet. You' better look one more time.'

Gerald ignored her and slipped the key into the lock and turned it. He opened the door and a deep tired voice said, 'You don't know me, so that's why I didn't give any name when you callin' out.'

Gerald asked him in.

'Missis Manson?' the man said.

Jessica stood and waited for him to continue.

'Look' like you' son reco'nize me a'right,' the man said. 'They call me Big Man. I come from you' 'usban' with a message.'

'Is he all right?' she asked.

'Right as ever, lady,' Big Man said reassuringly. 'I leave 'im down by Central with the police.'

'What's he doing there?' Gerald asked.

'Tryin' to bail out Missa Crossman, but they won't let 'im go.' Then Big Man turned to Jessica and said, 'Missa Manson ask' me to tell you that 'im's workin' on the bail, an' that 'im's personally a'right. Not to worry, 'im say.'

'Wha' 'appen to you' tongue a while ago?' Miriam asked pointedly.

'When you didn't open up the firs' time, I decide' to take a walk up the road an' come back later.'

'How did you get here?' Gerald asked.

'In Missa Crossman' van. I goin' back to you' father at Central when I leave you all.'

Gerald, Shifty and Fu questioned him closely about the state of affairs in Kingston. So did Jessica and Miriam.

Big Man gave them a vivid description of the violence and the fires and the activities of the police and the army and the volunteer reserve.

'Do you think it'll be over soon?' Gerald asked.

'Don't t'ink so personally meself.'

'When then?' Shifty asked.

'Not until they let go Missa Crossman.'

'So, wha' we got to hope for?' Miriam asked.

Big Man scratched his head and repeated the word 'hope', as though he felt it necessary to weigh up its importance before giving his answer, and then he said, 'The police do a stupid t'ing to arres' 'im, right under everybody' nose. The riot goin' go on for a long time. Look' like we find a leader we want. Once they let 'im go, t'ings boun' to cool down, nice as a ninepence.'

Miriam told Big Man not to go away, and went off to prepare a snack for him. It was obvious that she liked him. Gerald and his mother noticed that she had been looking at him intently while he was speaking, and they knew that he had impressed her.

'Have many people been arrested?' Shifty asked.

'A few well,' Big Man said.

'Many injured?' Jessica asked.

'I suppose so, ma'am. Plenty ambulance' 'bout the place.'

'D'you know about the curfew?' Gerald asked.

'Yes. I hear it mention' down at Central, but pure hell goin' pop when four o'clock come an' they don't let go Missa Crossman.' He looked apologetically at Jessica.

'What sort of hell?' she asked.

'Murders, ma'am.'

She shook her head and left the room. She looked tired and despondent. She dragged her feet as she always did when she was depressed and exhausted by anxiety and personal doubts.

'Were you stopped on your way up to us?' Fu asked Big Man.

'I know where to drive.' Big Man chuckled.

'But, weren't you stopped in Cross Roads?' Shifty said. He was deeply concerned.

'Didn't pass t'rou' Cross Roads at all.'

'What's the real position with Dad?' Gerald asked.

'Jus' as I tell you a while ago. Not'ing wrong. The police won't make 'im stan' bail for Missa Crossman, so 'im 'oldin' on 'til nex' never.'

'Will they give in?' Fu asked. His voice faltered.

Big Man scratched his head again, struck his forehead stylishly, and said, 'Wait an' see wha' goin' 'appen after four o'clock.'

6

After Big Man had eaten and left, Gerald, Shifty and Fu, and Jessica and Miriam went out to the back veranda and resumed their meeting. Gerald was clearly the centre of attention.

Jessica and Miriam came out, almost together, with the same first question.

'Where d'you know him from, Gerry?' Jessica asked.

'Yes, how come you know Big Man?' was Miriam's way of putting the question.

Gerald knew, now, that there was no other way out of the bottleneck he had squeezed himself into than to explain *everything*. He resolved instantly not to lie and not to tell only one half of the truth either. He told himself that, if his mother and Miriam wanted to know about Big Man, then they were also going to be told about the park, about Bag-'n'-Pan, and about the incident on Slipe Road.

And so he told them the whole story, everything in detail.

Jessica was so astonished, and pained, that all she was able to say when he had finished was, 'You're your father's own son, pig-headed and stupid, and a perfect fool for excitement.'

And from Miriam, 'You can pay for excitement wit' you' life, sure as lightnin' an' t'under drop out o' the sky.'

CHAPTER FIVE

1

Alexander Crossman was still being detained by the police at the Central Police Station.

Martin, Marcus and Big Man left the station at about three o'clock, under police escort, which they had not asked for but which they had been forced to accept. All three men were being taken to their respective houses, and on the way, the inspector who was in charge of the escort warned them, many times, to remember to observe the forthcoming curfew.

Big Man was the first to be dropped off. While driving to his house in Jones Pen, he, Marcus, Martin and the police escort saw the full horror of the rioting in the area. Big Man's street was strewn with splintered glass, mainly from the broken bulbs and shades of the street-lamps, with heaps of putrid refuse apparently from overturned Corporation garbage bins, and with the drifting, furtive groups of people who were looking into the gashes of shop-frontages, and breaking into and entering abandoned shops, and taking away large quantities of goods.

The presence of the police station-wagon did not deter the drifters; they continued their ransacking and aimless looting, and now and then they turned to taunt the occupants of the wagon; some made terrifying John Connu faces, some shouted, 'Let go the Chief!' and others flung empty cardboard boxes and milk-crates at the passing wagon.

'They'll be safely under lock and key after four o'clock,' the inspector said, leaning heavily against the dashboard and tapping the windscreen with his fingers. 'Safe and sound, and completely out of harm's way.'

'If you can catch them,' Big Man said.

'Don't you worry about that,' the constable, sitting beside him, said. 'We will, and how.'

'*And how* is right, Officer,' Big Man sneered.

'Think we won't be able to?' the constable asked him.

'Wish you luck,' Big Man said sarcastically, and pointed out his house to the driver.

As soon as the wagon drew up in front of Big Man's gate, someone rolled a large oil-drum accurately under the bumper and shouted, 'We want back the Chief!'

The inspector sat up and tried to catch a glimpse of the person who might have been responsible for the sudden assault, but he saw no one.

Big Man chuckled and said, 'Jones Pen duppy.'

'We can arrest ghosts, too,' the inspector said, returning Big Man's wry joke. 'Anyway, you're home now. Get out, and for your own good, remember to stay in and set a good example, and

103

don't let us catch you breaking the curfew. We'll be keeping an eye on you, Mr. Big Man.'

Big Man laughed. The familiar hunger marks, the bright white lines of dry spittle-foam, circled his parched lips and made his mouth look, at once, grotesque and comical. 'Wrong address, but don't tell them anyt'ing,' he whispered in Martin's ear.

Martin nodded.

Marcus looked puzzled.

'Tell 'im later,' Big Man told Martin and leapt out of the station-wagon.

The inspector, who was sitting in front, had not seen what Big Man had done, and the two constables in the back had also not been aware of his whispering; they were both looking at the messy disorder in the street.

In the meantime, the driver had got out and rolled the oil-drum on to the pavement and was standing watching Big Man going through the gate.

The next one to be dropped off was Marcus who had asked to be taken to his cousin's house in East Race Course. Before he got there, Martin told him what Big Man had said, and Marcus said, 'Same t'ing I doin', Missa Manson. I don't live in East Race Course. I don't even 'ave a cousin. Not even 'alf o' one, to save me life. Make them figure it out later.'

Martin remembered that Marcus actually lived at the bottom end of Kingston Gardens which was some distance away from East Race Course.

Like Jones Pen, East Race Course showed similar signs of the rioting and looting and the aimless groups of drifting people. Even some of the overhanging mango tree branches had been torn down and dropped in the streets, and there were a few deserted vans and trucks and motorcycles which had been over-turned and badly dented and scrapped in parts. One of the vans reminded Martin of Crossman's, and he asked the inspector, 'What about Mr. Crossman's delivery van?'

'It'll be all right in the station yard, I imagine,' the inspector said. 'If you want to take it away, you may.'

Marcus left the station-wagon without saying anything to

Martin or to the police, and ran through the open gate of a large ramshackle tenement yard.

Martin gave his right address and sat back as the station-wagon headed towards Cross Roads. When he got to his front gate, he tried, for the last time, to appeal for Crossman's bail. 'Won't you reconsider my request?' he asked.

The inspector grinned and said, 'Not a hope. Crossman stays where he is until we decide what to do with him, and until we've got control of all the mess and rioting.'

Martin slammed the wagon door and walked away.

'Got all the addresses?' the inspector asked the driver.

'All three, sir,' the driver said, tucking his notebook back into his shirt pocket.

'Hurry back to Central, now, eh?' the inspector said, shifting and resettling himself on his section of the broad front seat.

The emotion of the inspector's satisfaction transmitted itself directly to the driver who instantly over-revved the motor and swung the station-wagon round, with the tyres screaming over the asphalt and the alarm-bell ringing full blast, and hurtled down the middle of Half Way Tree Road. The wagon had travelled about four hundred yards, when six men sprang out of nowhere, threw six, long, bulky blocks of hardwood right across the road, and vanished. But the driver chose his path, in a split second; he swerved masterfully, once, and then a second time, and managed to avoid crashing into the central mass of the blocks; however, he ran over the edge of a stray one which had rolled away from the others and had got in the way of the left back wheel, and the impact of the tyre pinched and flicked the block of wood like a matchstick and sent it flying towards the pavement and into the expanse of a corrugated zinc fence, denting it deeply and making a clattering explosion.

The driver smiled self-congratulatorily, and the inspector said, 'Never had to deal with log-rollers before. Anyway, four o'clock won't be too soon, I don't think.' And he smiled too.

2

Martin, who was just about to open his front door, had his right hand outstretched to grasp the glass doorknob, when he heard the metallic bang down the road. He turned and ran back to the gate.

Gerald, Shifty, Fu, Jessica and Miriam also ran out of the house to see what the loud noise was about. Jessica and Miriam held on to Martin, welcomed him home and showed how relieved they were to see that he was in no way involved in the crash.

'Look at that fantastic dent!' Shifty said, craning his head and neck over Martin's shoulder.

'It's as big as an old-time bath-pan,' Fu said.

'Gosh! Look at it!' Gerald exclaimed.

'Where?' Jessica asked.

'In the fence,' Gerald said, 'between Movies and Sloppy Joe's.'

Jessica, Martin and Miriam saw the dent and nodded in astonishment at its size. Then Gerald pointed to the blocks of wood in the road.

'Roadblock or somet'ing,' Miriam said. 'But wha' crash' into it a while ago?'

Martin thought quickly about her question and the answer came to him in a flash. 'Could've been the police-wagon that brought me home,' he said in a matter-of-fact tone of voice so as not to cause any alarm. He looked at Jessica and smiled.

She asked, '*They* brought you home? When?'

'Just now.' Then he began telling them all about the police escort, while leading them back to the veranda. Later on, in the dining-room, he told them about the meeting in the park and about the visit to the Central Police Station; he also asked them if they got his message from Big Man. When Jessica mentioned that she and Miriam had heard about the incident in the park, Gerald knew that it was time for him to tell his father about his early morning exploits.

Martin listened and then he lectured Gerald on the dire consequences of deceiving his parents and on the stupidity of disobeying a simple order. Gerald hung his head in shame, and Miriam passed by and patted his shoulder. Martin realized that he had made his point, so he changed the topic and tried to see how he might distract Gerald.

'What do we do now?' he asked him, man-to-man.

'Like what?' Gerald said.

'Anything, other than sitting and waiting for the end of something that might go on and on for a very long time.'

'We could barricade ourselves in.'

Shifty and Fu beamed. They thought Gerald's suggestion positively inspired.

'And who's going to attack us?' Martin asked almost arrogantly.

'I t'ink we should take precaution', yes,' Miriam suggested.

'Good idea,' Jessica said. 'Even you, Martin, may be an unintended target, if things get worse while the curfew is on; and if not you, then the house. Besides, Cross Roads is bound to be an obvious trouble-spot.'

'What about it, Dad?' Gerald asked.

107

Martin pondered and then nodded.

They both got up, followed by Shifty and Fu, and went to the out-room. Gerald held the Rudge under his arm, leant it on the outside of the door and joined his father in searching for the necessary tools and materials for the job in hand. After they had selected everything they needed, Gerald put back the Rudge and closed the door.

The very first thing they did was to chain up the front- and side-gates, fixing each securely with a large foundry padlock. Then they cleared the edge of the veranda of all the potted plants and put them in the cool recesses under the house.

Because there was very little else to do after that, and because Gerald did not want the 'barricade preparations' to end so soon, he suggested that he, Shifty and Fu should nail a few battens across all the front windows, but Martin told him that that would only attract attention to the house, and would certainly tempt the rioters. But Gerald wondered about the wisdom of merely locking the gates and removing the potted plants and not going any further with the precautions.

'We've done more than enough,' Martin told him.

'What about the house itself?' Gerald asked. 'I mean: shouldn't we do something extra special about it?'

'It'll be bolted and locked on the inside, as usual, Gerry.'

'This afternoon and tonight aren't going to be *as usual*, Dad.'

'You'll be surprised.'

'We shouldn't take chances, Mr. Manson,' Shifty said.

'Nothing to fear, son. Not a thing. We'll be all right.'

'Because you're Mr. Crossman's best friend?' Gerald asked.

'Well, more or less everybody knows we've been working together for a long time.'

'Do *all* the rioters know that, Mr. Manson?' Fu asked.

'Not all, but I suppose news travels fast.'

They sat down on the second to the lowest tier of the veranda steps and stared round the front garden.

'I don't really like what's happening, you know, boys,' Martin said, staring into the multicoloured blaze of a bed of zinnias fringed with joseph's-coat. 'Like most people, I imagine, I'm always ready for a fight, but, at the same time, I dislike violence.

I often hope it'll help some people work things out for themselves, and yet deep down I don't believe it can.'

Gerald did not know what to say. He made up rapid successions of half-sentences but they remained locked in his head. He tried again and again, and the result of every attempt was meaningless and stillborn. Finally, he lost faith in his imagination and gave up entirely; he looked at the foundry lock on the chain round the posts on the front gate, and he shifted his gaze to the other lock on the side gate, and even then, he was unable to think of something to say to his father. He was more than mildly surprised to discover that he had not really given up trying; even though he had told himself that he had, the attempts were still being made in the distant recesses of his brain.

'Life's one long struggle for most people, boys,' Martin said, filling in the silence. 'And in a place like Jamaica, the struggle is very, very special. It has its own particular –'

'– But things are going to be better, aren't they, Dad?' Gerald blurted out nervously.

'Depends, son.'

'On the people, you mean?' Shifty asked.

'On *us. All* of us.'

A fire-engine clanged past, followed by a police car. The jangling noises of both vehicles smashed the tension of the adult exchange between Martin and the boys, and in a strange way, it helped to make them feel relaxed and, to some extent, detached.

Martin got up and brushed the seat of his trousers; Gerald did the same, at the exact moment and in a similar manner, so much so, that his movements seemed to be a conscious imitation of his father's. Then they walked slowly, and in step, round to the back of the house.

Shifty and Fu took the hint and went home.

As soon as Martin and Gerald saw Jessica and Miriam sitting together on the back veranda and looking out disconsolately across the vegetable-garden, they became tense again.

The final reminder came at five minutes to four. The announc-er's voice was low-pitched, deliberately slow and clear: 'The Island-wide curfew begins in less than five minutes from now. All members of the public are requested to stay indoors until six o'clock tomorrow morning.

'The curfew, (and I repeat) which will last all the way through from four o'clock this afternoon until six o'clock tomorrow morning, will begin in less than five minutes from now.

'We will be broadcasting other police messages and the usual news-flashes throughout the afternoon and evening.'

CHAPTER SIX

1

Four o'clock: A distinct lull descended over the riot areas throughout the Island.

Broome and the neighbouring rural districts were so quiet that they seemed wrapped in a Sunday morning hush. The villagers and the plantation workers who had remained behind and the other country people outside Broome had all gone into their houses and huts and wattle-and-daub compounds. The country roads were desolate, and only the occasional sounds of birds and restless farm animals broke the stillness.

Kingston was graveyard silent. The only movements in the streets were the smooth, almost silken, cruising patrols of the police transport and the throbbing scurrying of army trucks and fire-engines whose bells and sirens had been silenced.

Saint Andrew, too, was dead still. There were no cyclists, no motorists, no pedestrians anywhere.

Four thirty: And the silence persisted. Somehow, it seemed deeper and very nearly complete. There were, of course, the damped-down murmurs of music and intermittent announcements coming from the front rooms in certain houses, and even these were so muffled that they seemed to slide out from the houses like distant insect-sounds.

Four forty-five: The fire-brigade had successfully put out all the fires in the suburbs and in the commercial sections of the city, and the intense heat from the scorched buildings was shimmering upwards in endless streams.

The fires in Broome and in the outlying rural districts had also been put out.

Because of the quick and expert action taken by the firemen and their volunteer assistants in coping with the many sporadic outbreaks, vast, enveloping smoke-screens were rising and colliding and forming into an enormous grey-and-black blanket over Western Kingston and Lower Saint Andrew.

Five fifteen: There was a special announcement on the radio. The announcer said, 'Up to five minutes to four this afternoon, there were two hundred people injured in the rioting, twenty killed, and four hundred and twenty-six arrested in Kingston, Saint Andrew and in the rural parishes. Because of the excessive amount of arrests everywhere, certain public buildings are being used as temporary detention centres.

'Since the curfew began, an hour and fifteen minutes ago, there has been considerable calm in the corporate area and elsewhere. There have been no reports of arson or violence, and the rioters have disappeared from the streets.'

2

Five thirty: Gerald, his mother, his father and Miriam were sitting round the low mahogany table on the back veranda and not talking to one another. They had heard the last broadcast report and were now caged in their separate, dissimilar thoughts of despondency, anxiety and fear.

Gerald was silently wishing that something, *anything* at all, a loud noise, a sudden bang, would happen to shatter the unsettling feeling of suspension in mid-air which he was experiencing.

His mother was depressed about the whole tragic affair, and she was particularly upset about the news of the people who had been injured and killed.

Martin was also concerned about that, and he was thinking of Crossman and the outcome of the riot and about the effect it would have on the establishment of the Union.

Miriam was the only one of the four who was plainly panic-stricken; she was not normally the type of person to be so affected but the pressure of the circumstance and the intensity of her own personal involvement with it had caused her considerable anguish; for instance, she did not like the prolonged period of calm after the beginning of the curfew; she refused to be fooled by it because she was convinced that the rioting had not really been put

112

down, as the police seemed to think, and wanted her to believe; in fact, she had gone so far, in her private musing, as to imagine what it would be like when it flared up again, as she was absolutely certain it would. And characteristically, she was not thinking about her own welfare or her own physical safety; she was thinking of 'her family', of Gerald, Jessica and Martin. She had not once spared a thought for herself.

More than anything else, the news of the deaths and of the injured people was weighing heavily in the thoughts of all four of them sitting round the dining-table. At first, the horror of the news had seemed remote, as though it had come from another country and was about an event which they knew nothing of. But slowly, the report began to make its own terrible impact, and an overwhelming sadness settled firmly into the gloom already present on the back veranda.

3

Six o'clock: It was time for Alexander Crossman to be given his evening meal. The kitchen orderly opened the door of the cell, slammed the tray of food down on a three-legged pitch-pine table to the left of the door, stood with his elbows akimbo and glared contemptuously at Crossman who was lying on his side on a narrow cot under a high barred window. Crossman smiled and thought, 'You idiot! You're more of a prisoner than I am.'

The orderly pointed to the tray and said officiously, 'It won't come to you, you know.'

Crossman sprang off the cot and landed a few inches away from the orderly's highly-polished police boots. The orderly stepped back smartly, militarily, and placed his right hand on the baton in his side pocket.

Crossman smiled again and thought, 'You kitchen cowboy, you!' Then he walked to the table and stared down at his supper of cold corned beef slices, hard dough bread without butter, and a large mug of unsweetened hot chocolate.

The orderly chuckled and said, 'Station food soon knock some o' the big time pride out o' you.'

113

'You're doing all right on it,' Crossman said.

'I don't eat station food,' the orderly said, scowling angrily. 'We live good like anybody else outside.'

'Few people are living *good* outside,' Crossman said.

'Not my fault that.'

'In any case, you're not like anybody else outside. Are you?'

'Wha' you mean by that?'

'Work it out for yourself,' Crossman told him, and bent over the tray and made himself a bulky sandwich of the corned beef with two slices of bread.

The orderly did not reply.

Crossman went back to his cot and turned his back. He ate slowly, his mouth merely receiving the food mechanically, without effort, and without any noticeable enjoyment.

The orderly walked over to the window and looked out across the station yard.

'You don't wish that you was outside?' he asked.

'Trying to tempt me?' Crossman said.

'You' frien's not raisin' 'ell any more, you know. The curfew clip them wings, one time.'

'The calm before the explosion,' Crossman said, finishing his sandwich and getting up to fetch the mug of chocolate.

The orderly sat on the cot.

'Tell me something: why you all doin' it, eh?' he asked sympathetically.

'People get restless, fed up,' Crossman said.

'Wha' they want?'

'What people all over the world want,' Crossman said, draining the mug and handing it to him. 'A better break.'

'You t'ink they goin' get it one day?'

'The Union will help.'

The orderly got up, cleared the table and left the cell.

Crossman felt dreadfully depressed. Whenever he had to talk to anyone as wilfully unfeeling as the orderly, he usually ended up in a state of abject depression, and whenever the mood overtook him, he would try to dispel it by doing something that called for a display of sudden physical effort, however simple. And so, now, he had to do the same: he stood erect, stretched his arms above his head, brought them down and lifted them again, breathed in deeply and exhaled with the noisy panache of a champion weight-lifter. Then he did a number of knee-bends, and leant the whole weight of his body against the cool concrete wall; after that, he grabbed the bars of the window and looked out on to the station yard. It was deserted and splashed, in places, with the hot colours of the blazing sunset.

The stillness of the cell behind him and the stillness of the yard before him sandwiched his being and made him feel displaced, lost, *locked out*, because he felt neither enclosed within the walls of his cell nor near enough to the open air to sense the freedom of the yard. And it was then that he began to feel a tingling sensation crawling all over him like a swarm of tiny insects claiming the body of a dead beetle.

His head rang out and echoed with a scramble of darting visions of panic. He imagined accidents and crises and catastrophes and inevitable doom. And he saw fleeting appearances of, what he took to be, the death-masks of Martin, Marcus and Big Man, descending from nowhere and passing down a few inches before his eyes.

He shook himself, and still the scramble of visions kept sliding down in front of him. He rubbed his eyes, blinked, nodded vigorously, and they were there all the same. He forced his face into the space between the bars of the window and doubled the pressure of his skin on the rough metal, and, after a short while, the visions began fading away.

He fell limply away from the window, his body sagging against the wall, and dropped backwards on his cot. He felt purged, tired, sleepy. He closed his eyes and a rash of perspiration-beads covered his face.

4

Six thirty: Big Man was sitting alone in his small room; after the police escort had driven off, he had waited at the back of the yard in which he had been left; then he had walked down the street, about two hundred yards away, and slipped into his tenement room.

The waiting was telling on his nerves. He liked being organized and he particularly liked organizing things himself; he was unhappy about the way the riot had gone; it was almost leaderless. He wondered just what he was waiting for in his room. Who was going to give the signal to break the curfew? Who was going to start the upheaval again? Crossman was locked up. Marcus could be anywhere. Martin was sure to be at home with his family. The rioters were waiting. And the police and the army were everywhere, waiting too.

Big Man looked around the walls of his room. They were covered with scrapbook cut-outs from the *Gleaner* which he had selected carefully and had pasted up decoratively from time to time, especially during the long periods when he was out of work.

The cut-outs were mainly large pictures of dramatic scenes of all sorts, pin-ups of film stars, action photographs of cricketers like Learie Constantine, George Headley and Don Bradman, of international footballers, swimmers and mountain climbers, and exclusive photo-news reprints of the British, Danish and Swedish royal families.

And there he was sitting and staring at his private exhibition and feeling trapped and angry, sorry for himself, and thoroughly miserable. He closed his eyes and listened to the beating of his heart, then to the noises outside which were so distant and infrequent that they seemed to be coming from another world; they were the occasional rustlings of tree branches, the barking of a dog, and the familiar clucking sounds of wandering chickens. All subdued and remote.

Big Man had deliberately stayed away from his family who lived in the other rooms of the tenement. He had not been so quiet and inactive for a very long time.

Seven o'clock: Marcus was at home with his parents and his friends from the other rooms in the tenement yard. Like Big Man, he had waited for the police escort to drive away before going to his right address, about two miles away.

His parents were anxious, but they were resigned to waiting; and they were not necessarily waiting for the riot to begin again. They had been waiting long before the riot; they had been waiting all their lives, waiting for their many dreams to come true, waiting for their wishful fortunes to materialize and free them for ever from their dreaming and their wishing and their waiting.

'A man's got to learn to live with violence, same as with livin' with Gawd,' Marcus's father had said when the curfew began.

And Marcus's mother had agreed. 'In the breakin' is the wonderful bindin', my son.'

Marcus's friends were restless. He was their hero, but they wanted to go out and prove themselves too. Marcus had set them a daring example of his courage, and now the curfew was denying them the opportunity to match their craving for excitement and their stamina and intelligence with his; they were restless and waiting all right, but with a very marked difference from the way that Marcus and his parents were.

Marcus's father threw his favourite First World War service medal up in the air and caught it between his gnarled shaking fingers and said, 'We didn't 'ave a curfew in the trenches, Marcus. A man's got to learn to fight, constant like, for wha' he want, curfew or no curfew. If you don't fight an' mean it, then you don't win medals, son.'

'Only t'ing is,' Marcus's mother added, 'you can't take the pretty medals an' buy bread an' sugar, or take them an' start no Union either.'

The old man smiled ruefully, clasped his medal tightly and hid his hands under the flaps of his tattered and grease-stained khaki drill tunic.

Seven fifteen: Miriam was taking her time to lay the supper table; she found it soothing to linger over it, shifting a plate here, a fork there, rearranging the dish-mats in arc-like patterns, and then in ascending blocks along the length of the table, pulling out the chairs, tucking them back under the outer edge, and tugging and smoothing the tablecloth.

'What's for supper?' Gerald's voice came like a thunderbolt.

Miriam reacted accordingly. She held herself rigidly, sighed predictably, and then said, 'Exac'ly wha' you 'ave every Gawd Saturday night ever since I been cookin' for you' Mother.'

'That *spectacular* again?' Gerald teased her.

'I wonder if you know the amount o' starvin' people in the worl' who don't eat a single t'ing since mornin' light,' she began, but Gerald cut her off.

He said, 'I know. They'd love to have "a nice bowl of pepperpot soup right now".'

Miriam nodded. 'Correc',' she said and shuffled back to her kitchen.

Jessica and Martin came out to the back veranda and sat facing each other at opposite ends of the supper table. Gerald took his usual place, with his back to the sitting-room.

He watched his mother's fidgeting movements and tried to read her coded countenance: the wrinkled brow, the troubled eyes, the tense, pursed lips, the slightly damp fringe of tousled hair round her temples and down her cheeks. These were the obvious signs of her despondency, her depression, her own private torment.

Gerald then looked at his father. He was not what anyone might call 'depressed'; he was more or less anxious, less inwardly troubled, less deeply disturbed than someone utterly dispirited. Gerald was aware that his father was not a 'deep worrier' in the sense that his mother was. He was not being disrespectful, but he always expected his father to talk about the matter that was causing him anxiety, but not his mother. She bottled everything up inside herself; she held back her innermost thoughts and her actions, too.

Gerald felt sorry for her; on the other hand, he felt that he understood his father's unease.

'What d'you think of the curfew, Dad?' he asked.

'Seems to be working, son.'

'What d'you think, Mama?'

'It may be working, Gerry, but it can't go on for ever, can it?' she said primly, in her usual schoolteacher's manner, relying on the sure technique of half-statement and half-question to see her through the encounter.

'D'you think it's a good thing?' he pressed her.

'Well, at least nobody's being hurt or killed by the violence of the rioting.'

'So, it's good then?' Gerald concluded, forcing her to be positive.

'It's good as a temporary measure, as a stop-gap, Gerry,' she said, 'but we should all be pretty badly off if we needed a curfew to live out the rest of our lives.'

'Well, then,' he said, 'are people as strong as curfews?'

'I'm afraid not, son,' Martin said, 'even though curfews are man-made.'

'So we need curfews then?'

'Sometimes we do,' Jessica said.

'Like now?'

'Yes.' She closed her eyes.

Gerald looked away towards the back-yard.

Martin picked up the knife and fork set before him and made a 'balancing house-top', but as soon as he took his hands away, it wavered and fell with a resounding clatter.

Miriam brought in the supper, frowned disapprovingly at the sight of the disarranged knife and fork, and then began presiding over the table like a slightly bad-tempered high priestess.

Eight o'clock: After their supper of pepperpot soup, flour dumplings, crispy-crust bread and banana fritters, Gerald, Jessica, Martin and Miriam, who had all eaten halfheartedly, except Gerald, went into the sitting-room and waited for the latest news-flash which came over a few seconds after the hour: 'It's been reported that three adjoining two-storey houses in Lower Saint Andrew, which were badly damaged by fire and had been saved by the brigade and army early this afternoon from complete destruction, have since collapsed in a heap of charred rubble. The crash brought a number of people out to their verandas and gates, but no one went out in the street. The police were soon on the scene.

'The curfew: there have been no reports of incidents of civil disobedience, and the police expect continued full co-operation and understanding from the public for the rest of the curfew.

'Alexander Crossman is still being detained at the Central Police Station.'

The news-flash left everybody speechless.

Gerald and Martin got up and went to the front windows and looked out like trapped animals.

Miriam and Jessica sat where they were and stared at the wall facing them.

The room was a cage for all four; its one saving grace was its familiar size and personality.

'Can we go out on the veranda?' Gerald asked Martin.

'Feeling cooped up?' Martin said, sounding unusually sympathetic.

'Yes,' Gerald said. 'You, too?'

'We're all fenced in by the curfew, son. What's good for some *must* be good for all.'

'What about going out to the veranda? It's dark enough.'

Martin looked at Jessica and Miriam and said, 'No harm in it, I don't suppose?'

They made no comment.

Gerald opened the front door, and he and Martin stepped down on to the veranda and sat on the landing of the steps.

Jessica and Miriam remained in the sitting-room and gazed at the curved backs of the two sitting figures; for Jessica, they were her restless protectors, really no better off than Alexander Crossman who was also caged, and for Miriam, they were both overeager schoolboys. 'The Devil soon goin' fin' somet'ing for bot' o' you to do,' she thought as she looked at them with proprietorial tenderness.

The evening moved rapidly: from a streaky twilight purple to a cumulus grey to a smooth smoky blanket-gloom to darkness. Soon, Jessica and Miriam could make out only very small patches of Martin's and Gerald's white shirts, peeping through the night. The street-lamps were going to remain off, and the houses opposite had no lights on. The stillness was complete.

7

Twelve twenty, Sunday morning: Midnight had come and gone, and nearly everybody in Kingston and Saint Andrew had retired, exhausted, relieved, and some, hopeful. The police had relaxed their emergency supervision. All that were left on duty were the usual cruising night-patrols and the constables on the beat.

But there were four small groups of men moving about stealthily on the docks.

One group was being led by Marcus, another by Big Man, yet another by Horace, one of Marcus's closest friends, and a fourth group by a dock labourer who had seen Big Man leaving his room shortly before midnight and had followed him. The labourer's name was Preston.

Big Man had got tired of waiting for something to happen.

So had Marcus, who, incidentally, had had to escape the overpowering stoical attitude of his parents, and the nervous, egotistical chatter of his friends.

Unknown to each other, Big Man and Marcus had both left their rooms at the same time, Big Man alone, and Marcus with his friend Horace, and had headed for the docks. Their thoughts had been identical: to start something, anything. They had chosen the docks because they felt that the police would be concentrating their attention more in the commercial sections and in the suburbs, rather than along the waterfront.

The four men had each picked up a band of daring unemployed young men who were all in search of a leader with some sort of mission. Marcus's group and Horace's were wandering together through Number Three Pier. Big Man's and Preston's were close behind each other on Number One.

Marcus, Big Man, Horace and Preston and their groups met up in a customs-shed on Number Two Pier. Altogether, they were twenty men.

Big Man called them round him. He waved his arms and looked about the shed in an extremely business-like way; Marcus thought immediately of Crossman. It was clear that Big Man was taking over all the groups, in spite of the fact that each had a self-elected leader. When they gathered, he found a crowbar leaning against a barrel and began to clear an area of ground in the shed on which a small beam of moonlight was shining down through the glass roof, and he drew a crude diagram of the corporate area. First, he backed away and blocked in the three important piers in the dock area. After that he marked off Port Royal Street. He straightened up and said, 'That's the docklan'. Right?'

The group muttered its agreement. Though the single new group had been formed of four separate ones, it responded as if it had been *one* all the time, and this gave Big Man enormous confidence to carry on with his 'takeover'.

He hunched his shoulders and swung the crowbar like a pendulum and marked off three large rectangles, lying in a straight line immediately under Port Royal Street.

'Eastern Kingston,' he said, 'the business places an' such like, an' Western Kingston. Right?'

The group agreed.

He drew a small box and called it 'The Park', another and called it 'The Race Course', and a very much larger one and said, 'Lower Saint Andrew'.

Then he drew Cross Roads, Saint Andrew, and the hills.

'Good,' he said exultantly. 'The battlefiel' done now!'

'Wha' you t'inkin' 'bout?' Marcus asked.

'We goin' wake up everybody,' Big Man said, 'an' we goin' give them somet'ing to talk 'bout 'til mawnin' come an' dawn.'

'Like wha' so?' Marcus asked, trying to get him to be more explicit.

'Like a lil' excitement an' noise.'

'No fire business though,' Marcus stipulated. 'No fire settin' anyw'ere, at all!'

'No fire,' Big Man agreed.

'I been t'inkin' 'bout the excitement an' noise,' Horace said. 'The police still 'bout the place, you know.'

'An' the Up Park Camp people,' Preston said.

Big Man chuckled and said, 'We got the darkness to hide in, an' besides, we goin' move like duppy, sof' an' easy.'

'But wha' we really goin' do?' Preston asked.

Big Man looked at Marcus, and then back at Preston, and said, 'Cause some bot'eration an' a 'eap o' noise, mos'ly.'

'Sof' an' easy?' Marcus asked.

'Plenty *bangarangs*, sof' an' easy like,' Big Man countered.

He gave each regional leader a section of the corporate area to work on, and he emphasized the importance of carrying out the raids as quickly as possible. Horace was given a part of Western Kingston, half of the commercial section and the Race Course; Marcus got Lower Saint Andrew and Cross Roads; Preston, Upper Saint Andrew and the suburbs; and Big Man took Kingston Harbour, the dock area, Port Royal Street, a part of the commercial section and a part of Eastern Kingston.

' 'Ow we goin' cover the miles an' miles you give us?' Marcus asked Big Man with a trace of disenchantment showing in his voice which was low and husky with controlled excitement. Then he quickly added, ' 'Ow we goin' do it *sof' an' easy* an' quick?'

'We goin' drive,' Big Man said.

'Drive wha'?' Horace asked.

'Drive?' Preston exclaimed.

'Give 'im a chance,' Marcus said, calling them to order, and willingly playing the second-in-command to Big Man.

'We got to do the job quick an' bris',' Big Man began. 'Right?'

He got all-round agreement.

'Well,' he continued, 'we 'ave to travel fas' an' comfortable, an' wha' better to use?'

He paused for effect.

'Yes,' Preston said, 'but in wha', Big Man?'

'Easy t'ing, Preston,' Big Man said, throwing down the crowbar and pointing to Port Royal Street. 'We goin' get the bes' to do the job.'

He led the men out to the street, crossed it, and ran along the pavement at the head of the Indian file that had formed up behind him, quite naturally. He kept going at a brisk pace until he came to a motorcar showroom. He stopped and said, 'Take you' pick.'

'Wha' 'bout petrol?' Preston asked.

'Easy,' Big Man said. 'Take only the ones wit' a full tank, an' don't do no big deal wit' the engine w'en you testin' them.'

They broke into the showroom, tested the cars, pushed four outside and parked them in Port Royal Street. Then Big Man gave his final orders. 'Watch out for the police all you do, an' w'en the job done, dump the cars an' duck out o' sight an' go back to you' yard an' wait 'til mawnin' 'til the curfew finish. Now, wha' we do in the cars is this. Listen good.' He paused and thought twice before he announced his programme of provocation and incitement.

8

One o'clock, Sunday morning: Gerald had made many attempts to fall asleep; he had done several tiring floor-dips and knee-bends; he had covered his whole body and his head with the cool white sheet; he had sneaked out to the ice-pitcher and had drunk a glass of cold water; he had even tried to count all the names of his friends which began with 'Alex', 'John' and 'David'; and still he was unable to go to sleep. Finally, his restlessness was too much for him to bear, so he got up, dressed himself quietly and went out to the back-yard.

The entire surface of the yard, a part of the back veranda, and the front of the out-room were striped with intricate designs of moonbeams. The leaves and small branches of the overhanging trees had cast a fringe of filigree-shadows on the pavement between the veranda and the kitchen. Gerald stood and looked at the pattern moving gently up and down in a whisp of wind and wondered what to do, now that he was outside. He felt independent, adult and excitedly free. His excitement quickly faded into a sobering sensation of serenity as he realized that he was alone and unobserved. He could do exactly as he wanted. He could walk anywhere in the back-yard, do anything within reason, and nobody would reprimand him. He was his own man. He was in charge of his fate. He walked across the yard to the out-room and leant against the door. The image of his Rudge flashed into his mind's-eye. Why not? he told himself. Nobody would know; besides, it's something to do in the meantime.

So, he opened the door and took out the Rudge and parked it on the left pedal on a large embedded stone in the yard. He crept inside the house and collected his cleaning kit.

As he cleaned and polished the parts of the bicycle, the noises of the early morning, together with the strapping sounds of the cloth on the frame and fenders, whizzed round him and reminded him vaguely of a swarm of mosquitoes closing in on its target from a great height. He went on to imagine all sorts of fantastic likenesses between the objects in his actual setting and certain things in his imagination: for instance, his Rudge became, for a few seconds, a gigantic long-range rifle, then a Big Bertha, then a Haitian gunboat which he had seen near Port Royal, and again, a Bluebird-type racing-car; the out-room became an enormous aeroplane hangar, and the embedded stone, on which he had rested the pedal of his bicycle, the head of a dinosaur emerging from its sleep of centuries; and so it went on.

When he was finished, he led the Rudge round to the front garden and parked it on the veranda steps. He sat down and admired it, looking again and again at the gleaming metal parts, and comparing them, self-flatteringly, with the pictures he had seen of galactic clusters.

Quite suddenly a sensation of sadness came over him, as his thoughts strayed to the announcement of the people killed in the rioting. He shuddered. He hugged himself. And he closed his eyes. But the image of the prostrate and damaged bodies of the dead men and women presented itself clearly behind the shutters of his eyelids. His ears started to hear horrible dying cries of terror and pain; and he began to shake with the panic of his recollection, and his face and arms and legs became a tingling mass of goose-pimples.

He opened his eyes, but the haunting picture remained. The sounds continued.

He took a deep breath, held it for a long time, and then he released it very, very slowly.

The frightening sensation had imperceptibly slipped away from his mind and out of his body; the tension wore off quickly, and it seemed to him that something alien, something magical and powerful had oozed through his being and had lost itself in the morning air.

He fixed his eyes directly on the handlebar of the Rudge, and as he did so, he felt calm again. He remembered Shifty and Fu. The handlebar of his own Rudge became three handlebars, and the grips on each made him able to distinguish between his bicycle and Shifty's and Fu's.

Then the three handlebars melted back into one, and Gerald began admiring the sparkling lights which were radiating from the metal in front of him.

His attention strayed away from the Rudge, down to the locked gates, and out to the roadway. Again, he told himself, or rather, heard himself being told, 'Why not?'

But he replied honestly, 'The curfew's on!'

'Just for a short ride, that's all,' the voice said.

'No,' was the reply he heard himself giving. 'Not even for a short ride.'

'Not far, you know. Just up Half Way Tree Road and back.'

'No.'

He felt himself moving towards the front gate. His bicycle was ticking silkily beside him as he walked on in his peculiar state of self-induced 'hypnosis'. Then he stopped and lifted the bicycle over the low railings and eased it down on to the outside banking in the road. He felt himself climbing over the railings; he heard the padlock and chain rattling; and he felt his body jerk to a stop as he landed on the banking.

The spell dissolved completely.

Half Way Tree Road was empty and dotted and flecked with moonlight arcs and angles and deep shadows. He rode close to the gutter on the left side of the road, and he looked aimlessly round him, at the spectral lampposts, over the bulky aurelia hedges, into the gloom of the sequestered mango-tree rockeries, up at the shingles on the roofs. He had gone about two hundred yards when he came upon a heap of broken milk bottles. He dismounted neatly, looked at the glinting mess of jagged glass, lifted the Rudge clear of it and continued to ride up the road.

He listened to the distant, muffled barking of a group of dogs rummaging in the depths of a couple of overturned garbage-bins a few yards away on the right side of the road, and he counted the rasping volleys of cock-crowing coming from the Cross Roads circle behind him; volley succeeded volley, and bombarded one another as he rode slowly away from his house. At first, they sounded like warning blasts, but as they continued to break round him, they echoed like mere sound-effects being projected from the back of the stage at the Ward Theatre in a production of some play which was set in a country village.

He gazed down at the path which his front wheel was taking, seemingly all by itself, and he started to twist and twirl it, in and out of the shadows, in a series of futile attempts to skirt round them without crushing the edges, but the wheel crossed and checked and crossed again, and only managed to avoid running over the odd ones which were well separated from each other in any given combination of two or three masses of shadows. He had just failed to ride round the mammoth splash of a reflected lamppost when he heard an urgent screech of the tyres of a car as it braked a short distance away from his back wheel; he had not heard the car coming in his direction; not even the faint murmur of the engine had he heard. He did not look behind him. He leapt out of the saddle and dug his weight into the teeth of the sprocket to make a getaway as fast as he could, but, by the time he had driven both pedals a full revolution over, the surprised voice of a man rang out from the driver's-window of the car: 'Missa Geral', wha' you doin' out 'ere at this time o' mawnin'?'

Gerald recognized the voice immediatcly. He braked the Rudge, turned it round after releasing the rubber clamps, hopped off and ran to the front of the car. The driver had got out and was waiting for him at the side of the open door.

'Marcus!' Gerald said. 'What're *you* doing here?'

'Look,' Marcus said sternly, 'you better go back 'ome now. I come back later an' see you' father.'

'He's in bed.'

'An' you out 'ere?' Marcus was angry.

'Couldn't sleep. Anyway, what're you doing in a new car, and with all those people in the back? What's up, Marcus?'

'We doin' a job.'

'May I come along with you?'

'No. You can't. You mus' be mad. Get off the road an' go back to bed. The riot startin' up again. Police soon come an' fin' us talkin'. See you later.'

He jumped back into the car and raced up the road.

Gerald stood and watched the tail-lights disappearing into nothingness like frightened fireflies. Then he started back home; on the way, he recalled Marcus's startling parting words, '*The riot startin' up again.*' And their full impact struck him.

He lifted the Rudge over the front gate, climbed up and jumped down lightly after it and crept round the side of the house to the out-room.

As he was buttoning his pyjama-shirt just before slipping back into bed, he heard the first siren of three police cars which were to pass by, one after the other, in quick succession. After the third had passed, he decided to go in and wake his father, that is, if he had not already woken up.

Gerald left his bedroom and tiptoed into his parents' room. He leant over his father and whispered, 'Wake up, Dad.'

Martin's voice was firm, with no trace of sleep or drowsiness evident in it. He said, 'I know, son; it's started again. I heard them.'

'The police cars?'

'Yes.'

'Aren't you getting up, Dad?' Gerald asked, still whispering.

'To do what?'

'Dunno, Dad.'

'I've been lying here and thinking about what to do, Gerry.'

'Let's talk outside, Dad.'

'O.K.'

They tiptoed together into the sitting-room and afterwards

they went out to the front veranda and sat on the landing of the steps.

'Didn't take long, did it?' Martin said.

'Have you been expecting it?' Gerald asked.

'Haven't you, Gerry?'

'Suppose so.'

They did not say much more after that.

They sat and tried to imagine what was going on in the streets. They piled their own images of the scenes and the sounds, one on top of the other, and still their curiosity was unsatisfied, their speculations unstemmed.

It was quiet again.

A light breeze slithered through the tall Bombay mango tree at the edge of the left of the front garden and blew across the steps. The lapels of Gerald's pyjama-shirt flapped crisply against his cheeks and stung his eyelids, and salty tears filled his eyes.

He suddenly remembered his meeting with Marcus.

'Got something to tell you, Dad,' he said nervously.

Martin nodded absent-mindedly.

'Went for a short ride a while ago.'

'You must've been mad. Why?'

'Felt like.'

'What about the curfew?'

'I know.'

'What happened?'

'Met Marcus in a car, with some men in the back.'

'*Marcus*?'

'Yes. Said he'll see you later.'

'Stirring things up, is he?'

'Seems so to me, Dad.'

'Those police cars must've been chasing him!'

'Must have been.'

'For God's sake, don't tell your mother about your ride, eh?'

'O.K!'

Martin Manson's confused state of mind was very real to him at that moment; it was oppressive, and, as far as he had dared to think, nowhere near being cleared and ordered rationally by any 'counter-thoughts' which he could think of. Everything that was going on round him seemed haphazard and insoluble. It was becoming increasingly difficult for him to imagine what might come of his own high expectations, and Crossman's.

There's not even an easily recognizable 'enemy', he thought. It seemed to him that the people were actually fighting among themselves, destroying themselves, protesting against the presence of some festering sore hidden inside themselves and not against any definable outside cancer. Perhaps the cancer is inside our souls, and perhaps the people are aware of it, he suggested to himself.

The anger that had generated the upheaval was really a kind of exploding self-loathing, a self-directed assault, a self-destructive emotion which had broken out like boils throughout the unemployed and working classes in the society. When Martin thought of Marcus's most recent action, he saw it clearly as Marcus's desperate attempt to find and trap an elusive 'enemy'; Martin saw it as the futile search of an incensed man, a mad boxer perhaps, who had been locked in a room of mirrors which kept throwing back his multiple reflections at him while he continued to grapple with the complexity of identifying the *one* reflection which was not his own but his opponent's. In a sense, Marcus was shadow-

boxing with multiple reflections of himself; so were the others who were out with him in the streets, and Big Man, and all those who were thinking of defying the curfew.

Martin turned discreetly and looked to see what Gerald was doing; he was sitting quietly, tensely, and staring into the uncertain stillness of the morning; his face was masklike, oriental, almost too perfectly detached. For a very brief passage of time, Martin imagined that his son's countenance had become that of an old man's, passive and withdrawn. He tried to detect a reassuring trace of youthful excitement in it and he could find none. Then he roused himself out of his reverie and recognized Gerald's true state of mind: one of tension and ordinary boyish bafflement.

Martin felt relieved. He shifted his position on the landing and yawned. Gerald looked at him and smiled.

'We'd better go back inside,' he said tentatively.

'I might disturb your mother. Might as well wait a little longer.'

'Wait for what, Dad?'

'Not sure, son. Marcus maybe?'

'D'you think he'll come?'

'He told you so.'

'But maybe he won't. Maybe he can't.'

'True. They might've caught him.'

Not long after that, a police station-wagon sped up to the front gate and screeched to a shuddering stop; the bonnet dipped and bowed from the sudden braking, just like those of the light-bodied police cars in American gangster films; the four doors opened almost simultaneously and an inspector and three constables got out, slammed the doors shut and walked up to the gate.

Martin and Gerald were already halfway down the path.

'Early risers, I see,' the inspector called out.

'Like you, Inspector,' Martin said, reaching the gate and recognizing the familiar faces of the four men as they kept approaching in their characteristically self-confident semi-military manner.

'I suppose you worried men don't sleep during times of stress, eh?' the inspector said, hugging the top of the gate and looking like a good neighbour who had come to pass the time of day. He looked at the foundry padlock and the chain, and said, 'Yes. We're

131

passing through times of stress. No sleep for the good men who stand guard over the city.'

'I was just about to ask you,' Martin flung back jauntily, 'if you haven't had a break since you dropped me home.'

The inspector jerked himself to attention and said abruptly, 'Are you behind this fresh outbreak, Manson?'

Gerald stiffened. He drew close to his father.

'Would it take me to bring it about? You flatter me, Inspector.'

'What're you and the boy doing out here at this hour?'

'Your cars woke us up.'

'You could've stayed in bed.'

'I suppose we could have, but we chose to be out here. We haven't broken the curfew. Or have we?'

'You sure you haven't been seeing your two mysterious friends?'

'I haven't.'

'You haven't.'

'That's what I said.'

'We can't find them. They misled us about their addresses.'

'Seems natural when all's considered, Inspector.'

'Oh?'

'Well, you didn't ask them to give you their addresses; you merely offered to take them home.'

'*You* didn't lie. Why?'

'No reason to.'

'So *they* had reason to lie, had they?'

'Doesn't follow.'

'Right,' the inspector said, putting an end to the wry exchange, 'you see you don't break the curfew, and don't worry, we'll find your two missing pals.' He whacked the floppy seam of his left khaki trouser-leg with his officer's-stick and made a very formal about-turn, which his constables emulated like automata, and which made Gerald and Martin risk an admiring smile.

The station-wagon sprang away from the gate and roared up Half Way Tree Road.

'I hope they won't find Marcus,' Gerald said, watching the trail of ugly black exhaust-smoke as it rose up into a shaft of moonlight a few yards away from the end post of the front fence.

'Hope so, too,' Martin said, turning away from the gate and hunching his shoulders contemplatively.

'Marcus can fend for himself, can't he, Dad?'

'Spends his whole life doing so, Gerry. Sure he can.'

'Is he a good driver?'

'I'm certain he is.'

They went back to the landing and waited.

The minutes dragged on like heavy feet marking time in a small area of ground, steadily, evenly, monotonously. Gerald became less and less aware of his father's presence and so did his father of his.

And so, there they were: two islands apart in a sea of doubt and speculation and expectation. Their faces were set in blank expressions, in countenances which were concealing half-submerged pressures and anxieties.

Gerald was, ordinarily, very fond of his father's company, and the same could be said about his father where Gerald's was concerned, but, even in their present situation, it could be said that they were both sharing a common isolation. Their extremely close contact with each other had begun, quite early, with the ritualistic weekend games of 'bowl-for-bat' cricket matches in the back-yard, and with the traditional 'tennis ball' football sessions which were, more often than not, played against a high concrete wall in a clearing along Half Way Tree Road.

Gerald seldom ever thought of his father as his *father*; he was sometimes the 'old man' in the most affectionate sense of the expression, and sometimes he was just simply 'Dad', the senior partner, the adult companion.

Naturally, all the talk about the Union had made Gerald more inquisitive about his father's complex world; it made him grow even closer to the reality of what life meant outside his own sheltered world of Kingston College, the Scholarship Rudge, Shifty and Fu, and Miriam.

A mango fell from a nearby tree and dropped with a dull thumping sound. Gerald looked towards the spot. So did Martin.

Gerald knew that their isolation was threatened. He was not sorry. What would he say? Or would *he* say something first?

'How's school, Gerry?' the question came appropriately,

leisurely, rhythmically, like the beginning of the rehearsal of an ancient ritual.

'School's all right, Dad.' That, too, was as it should be, casual and direct at the same time.

And it was received trustingly.

'You must study hard, Gerry.'

'Yes, Dad.'

Pause.

'I saw you looking very preoccupied a while ago, Gerry. What d'you think of what's going on?'

'Nothing really.'

'No opinions of your own?'

'Nothing, Dad.'

'*Nothing?*'

'Well, I mean.' Gerald hesitated. 'You know what I mean.' He hesitated again. 'I mean it's not like what happens every day.'

'D'you know what it means, son?'

'That things are bad. Yes?'

'What else?'

'Things have got to change.'

'What else?'

'The Union will help do it.'

'And what about the Union, Gerry?'

'Well, it's a sort of protection for the working people. They can bargain better. They can raise themselves up a little bit, maybe.'

Martin smiled. 'A little bit, eh? And maybe.'

'A lot,' Gerald corrected himself.

'Even a little will be a lot, son,' Martin said, making his statement sound like an apology.

'But you do believe it will happen, don't you, Dad?'

'It has to.'

'How is it going to work?'

'Can't tell how it will work, really.'

'Like it works everywhere else?'

'I suppose it will work in our own way of doing things. After our own fashion, as in everything we do and work for.'

'Like the way it works in England, you mean?'

'Something like that, but more to our specifications, I hope,

134

son. More like the way we want it to develop and become our own set-up.'

'Yes, but how exactly?'

'Don't know yet. We've got to see how it shapes up. We've got to watch it come alive first. Legal status. Membership. Finance. Hard work. Things like that.'

'Will it take a long time to shape up?'

'Maybe. Maybe not. We'll have to wait and see.'

Pause. And then silence.

They had become islands again, and they waited.

9

Two o'clock, Sunday morning: Marcus, Big Man, Horace and Preston were still driving around, even though they had been chased from time to time and had been trapped once or twice by roadblocks which they had managed either to bypass or bludgeon their way through at the last moment. But in spite of the obvious risks, they had kept on escaping from the pursuing police- and military-transport wherever they appeared in their respective areas of operation.

Big Man and his six companions had carried out their acts of provocation and harassment in the streets in the vicinity of the docks and in the semi-residential sections of Eastern Kingston; they had torn down shop signs, shattered empty milk bottles, and 'fixed' motorcar horns so that their incessant klaxoning would, as Big Man had said, '...wake up Gawd Awmighty 'Imself an' make 'im bawl for mercy.'

Horace and his four passengers had been doing very much the same sort of thing in the commercial section and in Western Kingston and in and around the Race Course. They had also daubed all the statues in the park at Parade with red paint which they had taken from a ransacked hardware store.

Marcus had succeeded, almost single-handedly, though his five helpers had done their own share of protest work, in emptying most of the garbage-bins along Lyndhurst Road and Maxfield Avenue and some in the other main roads in Lower Saint Andrew.

Marcus had stayed away from Cross Roads because he intended to call on Martin on his way back to Kingston. But he had gone into the suburbs above Half Way Tree Road and had caused sporadic disturbances there.

Preston and his five men had tackled Upper Saint Andrew and the villages in the foothills. Most of their activities were confined to angry shouting and singing the new 'Crossman song of praise', together with 'fixing' motor horns and overturning garbage-bins.

Naturally, the whole corporate area was, more or less, aware of what was happening; those people who had not heard the actual marauding noises, had received telephone calls from their relatives and friends who had, and of course, there was the usual passing on of the news over the neighbouring side-yard fences.

Two fifteen: Marcus felt that it was time to turn back and head for Cross Roads, but as soon as he was about to do so, he spotted a police car coming up behind him. He looked in the rear-view mirror a second time and sized up his chances of escape; he glanced down at the fuel gauge and hurriedly worked out how far he could still continue to go on the petrol he had left; and, finally, he read the speedometer which was registering sixty miles an hour: he decided that he was prepared to take on his pursuers and that he would be able to shake them off in next to no time.

He bobbed up and down on his seat, hunched his shoulders determinedly, expertly, and renewed his grip on the steering-wheel. The needle of the speedometer climbed easily from sixty to sixty-five to seventy to seventy-five; and the police still kept coming. Marcus smiled a wicked smile. His five passengers were silent and rigid with the feeling of suspense which was evident round them in the overheated cabin of the car. The needle climbed to eighty. The body of the car was firm and rattleproof; nevertheless, it shuddered slightly once when Marcus drove over a PWD repair-patch in the centre of the road while he was looking in the rear-view mirror.

The police car seemed to be gaining. Marcus quickly calculated the decreasing distance between him and his pursuers and he resolved instantly to turn off at the next intersecting road. He steeled himself for the turn, looked in the rear-view mirror once again, and smiled wickedly. The police were very close now. The intersecting road shot into view but Marcus was unable to negotiate the turn in time. Yet he knew what he had to do. He deliberately sacrificed his bolting top-speed and suddenly slammed on his brakes. The police car rammed him brutally and sliced off his back bumper and smashed into the soft metal of the boot. As the impact occurred, Marcus wrenched his steering-wheel violently and got out of the path of the collision, while dragging the police vehicle along with him for a short distance. Then he zigzagged his front wheels, detached the boot and shot away from the badly damaged and immobile police car.

Two thirty, Sunday morning: The four-part provocation tours had had their desired effect. The curfew had been challenged; it had been defied. Many of the streets in the corporate area were dotted with drifting groups of shouting, singing and gesticulating men and women who were shrewdly keeping near to their houses and deftly disappearing into the protective recesses of the moonlight-shadows along the pavements and side streets whenever the police or military came on the scene.

Big Man, Horace and Preston had all dealt with their respective pursuers in one way or another, and had ditched their cars in odd places along the way, and had gone home safely. Marcus had dropped his men off, too, and was circling back towards Cross Roads, picking and choosing all the available quiet short-cuts where he would not run into any of the patrolling police cars and army lorries. When he got to the top of Arnold Road and South Camp Road, which was within a mile or so of the intersections of Cross Roads, he drove the car into a thick clump of bougainvillaea at the entrance of a disused botanical nursery. He then walked and ran the rest of the way to Martin Manson's house.

But there was a great shock in store for him, something that he had not bargained for, something that he and Big Man had not planned or even hoped would happen.

As he got to the top of the rise on South Camp Road and was about to run down the gradient into the bowl of the intersecting roads, he saw huge clouds of smoke rising from some of the buildings in Cross Roads.

There were police cars, lorries and fire-engines parked everywhere, and strangely enough, there was also a large crowd of people standing around and watching the spectacle; Marcus noticed that the spectators were not being moved on or arrested by the police, and so he crept cautiously among them and stood and gazed up at the blaze. It had not yet gone beyond the central bowl of the intersections, which meant that it was not near to Martin's house on the Half Way Tree Road, but there was always the chance that it would spread fast if it were not controlled substantially within a matter of minutes.

Marcus looked round him and counted the places which were alight: the market sheds, three Chinese shops, a drug-store and a hardware store. The flames were brilliantly lively; they were licking the woodwork and the dry papery contents on the shelves and those in the shop windows with a crisp, crackling venom. The sounds were harsh, seething, tearing, rasping. The many exposed small objects in the burning rooms and stalls and shop entrances looked like sacrificial offerings, well-positioned and terribly lost. Certain shapes, like the cylindrical forms of condensed milk tins, canned food and piled rolls of toilet tissue, seemed like human heads on fire, remaining motionless and then falling slowly backwards as they were burnt by the howling blast around them.

Marcus was becoming mesmerized by the leaping yellow and black colours massing in front of him; the yellow flames leapt and subsided, and the black smoke oozed through the hot fissures of the burning structures and belched itself into the open air and billowed everywhere. The moonlight had taken second place to the two dominant colours: the black and the yellow; in fact, they had made the very early hour seem later than it was, a premature dawn, a sparkling, deceptive light and shade.

There were urgent whispers in the crowd, and Marcus heard someone saying, '…an' it could be another madman, yes, like Burn Down Cross Roads. You remember wha' 'im did do? I can't forget wha' Missa Burn Down Cross Roads cause in this same Cross Roads 'ere.' And Marcus remembered, too. The man's nickname was indeed Burn Down Cross Roads, and he was possibly the most celebrated arsonist in the West Indies. He had nothing to do with this fire, Marcus felt sure. He told himself that this must have been set off by someone else, or caused by some other agent, perhaps by an electrical fault in one of the buildings. He knew that none of the touring groups would have done it; they could not have; besides, Cross Roads was *his* area.

He withdrew from the crowd, leant against a lamppost and wondered who or what could have caused the fire. While he was pondering the question, a woman standing to the left of the lamppost pointed towards the post office and shouted, 'Look, the Broome people comin'!'

Marcus looked quickly and saw a truckload of men moving slowly towards the centre of Cross Roads. Painted on the head-board above the cabin and across the bonnet in large white letters were the words BROOME SUGAR ESTATE.

The police and the soldiers and the firemen acted instantly; they turned from their fire-fighting and hurriedly prepared a barricade between themselves and the approaching rioters.

The crowd scattered like struck glass marbles.

Marcus tried to hide behind the lamppost but he soon shifted round to the back of a nearby waist-high concrete parapet and ducked out of sight. He wanted to witness the imminent clash; he felt he had to, because, as far as he knew, there had not been an actual encounter between the police and any of the rioting groups either before the curfew or during the present outburst of defiance.

The police-, fire-brigade- and military-barricade of clustered vehicles, with all the available ladders and safety fences placed bumper-to-bonnet and with the lengths and coils of hose-piping filling the odd gaps between the street and the pavement, was now ready.

The Broome truck had stopped in front of the point-duty policeman's circular stand.

Both sides were motionless. Neither showed the slightest sign of making the first move.

The only sound in Cross Roads was the hiss-and-crackle of the fire.

Suddenly, a number of heads and shoulders peeped over the back of the truck, and a shower of stones was released with a slicing *whoosh*; it landed on the metal parts of the fire-engines and army lorries with a deafening clatter.

Two firemen replied by aiming one of the 'live' hoses straight at the bonnet of the truck.

The truck reversed out of the range of the pelting flood of water.

The firemen turned off the flow.

The heads and shoulders appeared again, and this time, there was an onslaught of half-bricks and bottles which splintered itself helter-skelter on the broad front of the barricade.

Once more the two firemen answered with an accurate blast of hydrant water.

Marcus dared to peep over the concrete parapet. What he saw baffled him: two opposing front lines, but no single person in full view. Something else that seemed strange to Marcus was the fact that nobody had been shouting or giving orders or uttering any threats or exhortations. Both sides were dead still.

Marcus shook his head, ducked down behind the parapet, and waited.

Then the third assault came: a javelin-spray of short sugar-cane stems which bounced off the barricade and dropped on the asphalt in a series of irregular thuds.

The firemen did not reply.

A few minutes elapsed, and the truck backed away, stopped, turned right round, and drove slowly down Slipe Road.

The firefighters went back to the fire, and Marcus, again, shook his head and walked cautiously away. He hugged the fences along the side of the road and went straight up to Martin's house. When he got there, he found all the family standing at the front gate, looking out at the awesome scene in Cross Roads. Shifty and Fu were also there. Marcus jumped over the fence and took Martin aside.

'Did you see wha' 'appen a while ago, Missa Manson?' he asked.

'I saw a part of it,' Martin said. 'I heard the woman's shout and I saw the front of the truck for a short time, until it backed away. But I saw the stuff they threw.'

'The Broome people carry on like duppy 'pon night raid,' Marcus said flatly, unbelievingly.

Martin chuckled quietly.

Marcus continued, 'I did wonder where they was hidin' out since the curfew, you know.'

Martin folded his arms and looked down at his bedroom slippers. 'What about the fire, Marcus?'

'Who do it, Missa Manson?'

'Don't know,' Martin said. 'You didn't, did you?'

'No.' Marcus frowned.

'Why're you so concerned?'

'Jus' wonderin'.'

'Why?'

Gerald, Shifty and Fu joined them.

'What've you done with the car, Marcus?' Gerald asked.

'I dump it by Arnold Road top.'

'So you weren't caught then?'

'No.'

'What happens now?'

'Better ask you' dad.'

Martin raised his shoulders and dropped them hopelessly. He had not the heart to tell Marcus the truth about his thoughts; the whole upheaval had been a nightmare of futility up to that moment; the incident with the Broome truck had underlined the uselessness of the riot. Nothing that had happened had yet convinced Martin of its usefulness, its real political purpose, its dynamic. Crossman was out of the way. The people were virtually leaderless. The second outburst of violence and commotion was like the first, nervous, diffuse, unconsolidated. And more than that, the very nature of the upheaval was physically enemyless, though it certainly had a rootedness, a connection, a unique historical and psychological definition and momentum.

Martin thought of the Island's very early years of slavery, then he thought of its colonial status, and he recalled words like 'exploitation', 'inferiority' and 'despair'.

'Wha' you t'inkin' 'bout, Missa Manson?' Marcus asked, after he had waited to hear what Martin would say to Gerald's question.

'Nothing,' Martin said. 'I suppose the next thing is the end of the curfew, perhaps. I don't know.'

'Wha' 'bout Missa Crossman?' Marcus asked.

'We've just got to wait and see, haven't we?' He smiled in an attempt to hide his inconsolable sadness. Then he embraced Gerald and held Marcus's arm and led them back to Jessica and Miriam who were still watching the fire.

Shifty and Fu attached themselves to Gerald and walked, in step, behind him.

11

'Can we give them the slip and go and look for Big Man?' Fu suggested, while Martin, Jessica, Miriam and Marcus were walking back to the front veranda.

'You mad or what?' Shifty whispered.

'Why Big Man?' Gerald asked.

'Well,' Fu said, 'we know that Marcus is O.K.; he's here. Let's check on Big Man; besides, it's something to do.'

Gerald narrowed his eyes. He was all for stepping up the excitement.

'What about the curfew, Fu?' Shifty asked. 'And the police? And our old people?'

'That's just it,' Fu said. 'If we can get away with it, it's something really fantastic to do.'

'Madness,' Shifty said, shaking his head and lapsing into silence.

'Wait a sec.,' Gerald said.

'What?' Fu asked hopefully.

'Do we know where Big Man lives?'

'We can ask Marcus,' Fu said. 'Sort of casual like, if you know what I mean.'

'Right then,' Gerald said. 'Let's. You do it, Fu. Sort of casual like.' He paused. 'If you know what I mean?'

Shifty laughed quietly.

Fu was ready for the challenge.

Marcus was sitting on the top step of the veranda and talking to Martin, Jessica and Miriam.

Fortunately for Fu, Jessica and Miriam soon got up and went inside the house.

Fu stood in front of Marcus and said, 'Do you think Big Man will come to see Mr. Manson?'

'Shouldn't t'ink so,' Marcus said, and looked at Martin for confirmation.

Martin shook his head.

'Maybe it's because he lives too far away,' Fu suggested. 'Where does he live?'

'Somewhere in Jones Pen,' Marcus said. 'Where exac'ly, I don't know for sure.'

'Not even the street?' Fu asked.

'Could be near where the police escort dropped 'im off yesterday, near Miller Street.' Marcus turned away from Fu and continued his conversation with Martin.

Fu went back to Gerald and Shifty, and together they planned their escape.

12

Four o'clock, Sunday morning: The families in the three neighbouring houses were all asleep; only Gerald, Shifty and Fu were awake in their rooms. Shifty and Fu were waiting for Gerald's signal.

He dressed quickly, slipped out of his bedroom, got his bicycle, and whistled *John tu-wit* softly across both side fences.

Four twenty-five: Miller Street was not difficult to find. It was one of the popular streets in Jones Pen. The boys rode their Rudges like experienced patrol men, Gerald in the lead, and Shifty and Fu evenly spaced out behind.

They had carefully avoided going through Cross Roads. And they were skilful in finding clear paths for themselves among the litter and broken glass scattered everywhere. They had been lucky not to have run into any police cars or to have been spotted by the constables on the beat.

The tenement buildings along Miller Street were very nearly all alike. The barbed-wire fences were the same. Even the fetid smell, all the way down the street, was similar, from house to house.

'How do we know which is Big Man's yard?' Gerald called over his shoulder.

'We might see somebody,' Fu said.

'We might be seen too,' Shifty said.

'We can cope,' Gerald assured them both.

They were excited by their daring adventure.

'Hey!' a voice rasped some distance in front of them. 'Wha' you boy-pickney doin' out in the street?'

Gerald, Shifty and Fu sensed that there was no threat or menace in the person's voice, merely concerned surprise, and so they headed towards the spot from which it had come.

An old man appeared out of a ragged clump of croton and aurelia bush, shook his fists at the boys and said, 'You' goin' get lock' up if you don't look sharp an' fin' you' yard!'

'We're looking for Big Man's place?' Fu said, making his reply sound like a question, extremely courteously put, and as calculatingly smooth as he could manage.

The man was impressed. 'Number 22,' he said, sighing disapprovingly.

Fu thanked him, and he and Gerald and Shifty went off to find the address.

Number 22 was a typical tenement yard. It was vast and cluttered with very shabby one- and two-room wooden houses. The yard was quiet. Only a dripping standpipe could be heard in the distance. There were several small shadows sprawled across the ground. Some were moving gently; others were motionless like deep grey stains.

The boys parked their bicycles and started towards the nearest house.

Suddenly, the yard came alive with voices and movement, and in an instant, there was a throng of people milling about and sweeping down on the three intruders.

Gerald recognized Big Man in the centre of the mass.

'Missa Geral', wha' you doin' down 'ere?' he asked, while waving to the people and trying to get them to calm down.

'We wanted to see you,' Gerald explained. 'To see if you were all right.'

'Missa Manson know you' 'ere?'

'No. We slipped out.'

Big Man laughed. The people murmured among themselves and smiled at the boys.

Gerald looked around him, and he wondered at the humble surroundings and at the many signs of overwhelming poverty. So did Shifty and Fu. They had never before come face to face with so much widespread neglect, dispossession, and underprivileged life.

Big Man noticed the boys' concern, and he said, 'We live rough in Jones Pen, you know, but it can't las' for ever.'

The boys nodded.

The people were dressed in ancient rags and they looked destitute and hungry and forlorn. But Gerald also recognized that their poverty was not as important as their impressive show of courage and dignity. But then he wondered what use that would be to them in their condition.

'We goin' to win one day soon come,' a tall woman said, spreading her arms wide to take in the crowd of people round her.

Another woman said, 'Our Big Man 'ere goin' 'elp us to make a move.'

Big Man smiled. 'They dependin' on me the same way I dependin' on Missa Manson an' Missa Crossman,' he said, staring first at Gerald and then at Shifty and Fu.

'Were you out with Marcus earlier?' Gerald asked.

'Had me own motorcar,' Big Man said, 'an' I had me own territory to cover.'

'You didn't set fire to Cross Roads?' Shifty asked.

'No, man,' Big Man said.

'You haven't heard then?' Fu asked.

'No.'

Fu looked at Gerald, and Gerald took over. He told Big Man about the fire. The people gathered round and listened spell-bound. When he was finished, an emaciated old man, dressed in a tattered military tunic and cricket flannels and looking very much like Bag-'n'-Pan, hawked and spat, and said, 'We might be poor an' miserable, but we can use matches like the nex' man, but we didn't; none o' us did. In fac', in a way o' speakin', all we got is matches. We got poverty, but we got plenty fire on our side, if we want to use it.'

Big Man patted the old man's shoulder. Then he led the boys towards his room. 'You got to go 'ome quick,' he told them.

He lit his oil lamp and showed them his pictures on the walls round his room.

Gerald recognized his favourite film stars. Shifty gazed at the action photographs of Learie Constantine, George Headley, and Don Bradman; and he lingered over the ones of Jesse Owens and the other American athletes. And Fu wandered round the room and compared it with Bag-'n'-Pan's. Big Man's was larger and more interesting because of the pictures, but it was just as dusty and poverty-stricken.

'Time to go,' Big Man declared, and he hustled them out of the room and across the yard.

The people were still there. They were sitting on the ground and staring at the emptiness of Miller Street. Their eyes glistened in the moving moonbeams, and their expressions were vacant and hopeless. Yet, it was their way of waiting and hoping.

Again, the boys showed concern, as they began to walk among them; the boys' faces looked worried and questioning. Big Man hovered over them and said apologetically, 'I know that we need more than a Union, but even a Union is a start for those who workin'.'

The boys said nothing. And Big Man added, 'Wha' we really need is a proper country, with people who will look after people, jus' because people is people, an' nothing else.'

Gerald, Shifty and Fu waved goodbye, and Big Man saluted. A few of the people behind him shouted, 'Ride good!' and the others waved listlessly.

PART THREE

THE AFTERMATH

CHAPTER SEVEN

1

Dawn, Sunday morning: It was a very calm, seemingly ordinary break of day, taking into account the barrage of harrowing events which had preceded it and which had actually ushered it in. The fire in Cross Roads was finally put out some time after five o'clock and the crowd watching it, who had returned after the Broome attack, had dispersed without police supervision; nobody had been arrested. The drifting protest-groups had also left the streets in the corporate area and were all back in their houses long before dawn.

And yet there was something raw, something sore and tender and red-eyed about the look of the new day. Even the early bird-song and cock-crow sounded tentative and half-hearted. Very few people were sleeping really soundly; quite a number were lying awake and dawn-dreaming.

In a sense, it was a time for fitful sleep, wild imaginings and dark presentiments. The stillness and the hollow feeling during the hour before and the hour after sunrise, of any day, is a period of doubt and suspicion and subtle fears for a people living under stress. If there is the intervention of hope, it usually comes later on when there is movement, when there is chatter, when there is some sort of distraction, some sort of planning for the day ahead, in spite of the futility and unhappiness of the day before.

Seven thirty: The pealing of church bells echoed in familiar places and began to mark the proper start of the traditional Sunday, and slowly the feeling of community confidence stirred and imperceptibly asserted itself. An hour and a half had passed and the curfew was over; and nowhere was there a rush to celebrate its passing; nowhere was there a declaration, however personal, of release or jubilation. It was as though the curfew had never been imposed.

In the houses in Lower Saint Andrew and in Western Kingston, breakfast fires were being kindled in the age-old way: with chipped pitch-pine pegs and a scattering of coal heaped within a stand of three or four soot-scarred bricks, and under the watchful gaze of a grandmother, or of a young girl who was quite new to the ritual, as she leant forward on her knees and blew the reluctant sparks alive in a far corner of a cluttered tenement back-yard.

In the middle- and upper-class homes in Upper Saint Andrew, fires of another kind were being lit, and the smell of attractively packaged coffee would soon be filling cool, spacious tiled kitchens.

2

Eight o'clock: Jessica, Martin, Gerald, and Marcus, who had slept at the Mansons' house, were sitting down to a simple breakfast of ackee and salt fish, hard dough bread and Blue Mountain coffee, and were being diligently 'mother henned' by a confidently padding Miriam whose white apron shone with an austere symbolic brilliance which was her badge of office and clearly hinted that she was once more the protector of all she served and surveyed within the household, upheaval or no upheaval.

After breakfast, they waited in the sitting-room for the eight-thirty news.

The announcer began by saying: 'The curfew ended two and a half hours ago. The state of emergency continues. It is believed that it will remain operative for an indefinite period – at least, for the duration of the coming week, maybe for a longer time.

'And now, the special announcement. We have just received the following message from the Commissioner of Police; it reads: "Alexander Crossman, who has been detained at the Central Police Station since the outbreak of the rioting yesterday, is to be released some time later today".'

Marcus got up and shook Martin's hand excitedly. Both men smiled warmly at each other. Gerald stood and rubbed his hands together and clapped them rhythmically again and again. Jessica and Miriam nodded their approval and relief.

'I wonder wha' time they goin' let 'im go?' Marcus said almost breathlessly.

'Did you notice that that was not mentioned?' Martin said coolly. 'There's a very good reason for that. No demonstration. No fuss. Just a quiet release, and that's that.'

'Makes sense, Dad,' Gerald said.

'For the police, yes,' Martin said.

'But not for us?' Marcus wanted to know.

'Well,' Martin said, hesitating slightly, 'we could make some capital out of it for ourselves. Couldn't we?'

Marcus smiled.

'They might slap him back inside,' Gerald suggested.

Jessica frowned at the way he had expressed himself. Miriam sighed in mild censure.

'We've got to take that chance,' Martin said, his former expectations springing back to life. 'We've got to arrange it, of course.'

'How?' Gerald asked.

'Wha' you t'inkin', Missa Manson?' Marcus said.

'We'll go down to Central and wait around,' Martin proposed.

'Missa Crossman' van still down in the yard,' Marcus said, hoping that the information might be useful in some way to Martin.

'Couldn't you ring up and ask the desk sergeant?' Jessica asked.

'He wouldn't give us the time of day,' Martin said. 'But I could try. Why not?'

'Better we go, Missa Manson,' Marcus said. 'That sergeant an' we don't 'gree at all. Might even block you on the phone, before you start.'

'May I come along with you, Dad?' Gerald got in his crucial request early.

'Can't see why not, son,' Martin said.

Jessica stiffened. Miriam coughed.

'He'll be all right,' Martin assured them both.

'What about Shifty and Fu, Dad?' Gerald asked.

'If their parents say it's O.K., then it's all right by me.'

Gerald smiled. 'When do we go?' he asked.

'Sooner the better.' Martin slapped the back of Gerald's head affectionately and left the room.

After Martin, Marcus, Gerald, Shifty and Fu had set off, closing the front gate noisily behind them, Jessica and Miriam sat on the back veranda, and, in their usual intuitively feminine way, mused aloud about the state of affairs.

'Look suspicious to me, as if they want to start it up again,' Miriam said. 'Missa Crossman comin' out o' the station lock-up an' goin' go right back inside quick o'clock, if I know wha' 'pon Missa Manson' min'.'

'Martin's a determined man,' Jessica said, folding her arms, pouting her lips and furrowing her brow, as she assumed her 'teacher's attitude', which meant that Miriam could expect to hear a monologue of highly personal insight and prophecy.

But, ironically enough, *that* was to come only from Miriam's replies.

To Jessica's statement, she said, 'The law is a very determine' t'ing, too, you know.' And she hung her head like a tragic heroine.

'Somehow, I don't think that Martin'll try any high-pressure tactics just now, Miriam, especially as the boys are with him.'

'Wha' I say is this: if time ripe, it *ripe*, w'et'er the boys wit' Missa Manson or no.'

'I don't think it would serve Martin or Crossman any good purpose to defeat their own programme.'

'Programme come w'en it come, defeat or no defeat. W'en programme call, you got to answer the call an' talk back quick an' bris', or it get col' 'pon you' plate, 'til nex' never.'

'It might never come again, you mean?'

'Nex' never.'

To that, Jessica merely nodded philosophically.

CHAPTER EIGHT

1

Martin and Marcus were passing Movies in Cross Roads with Gerald, Shifty and Fu following close behind them and leading their Rudges which they had asked Martin's permission to take along. All five of them were looking around in silent astonishment at the after-effects of the rioting and the fire.

The aftermath bore terrible scars everywhere; some of the traces of the destruction were slight, and others were total and terrifying to look at.

The hoardings, ticket-office, and a part of the front wall of Movies were very considerably damaged. Many of the picture displays had been slashed and torn down. The TODAY signs had been scratched away, and the eyes of some of the actors and actresses in the glossy photographs on show had been gouged out.

The dent in the fence between Movies and Sloppy Joe's seemed to Gerald, Shifty and Fu to be much larger than it had appeared the day before. Gerald called his father's attention to it and told Marcus how it happened, and then he looked around to see if he could spot any of the blocks of hardwood which had been thrown in the roadway; he searched for the one that had dented the fence, but he could see no trace of it, or of the others. What he did see was the torn fragments of a few TOMORROW, NEXT WEEK and COMING SOON signs, pasted erratically over the dent in the fence.

The buildings which had been on fire earlier were a grotesque sight. The burnt-out windows and doors, the scorched concrete foundations and walls, the blistered and gnarled paintwork and the ruined goods and furniture reminded Gerald of a scene in a cowboy film in which a whole thriving new frontier city had been razed to the ground by repeated Indian attacks and transformed overnight into a forgotten ghost town.

He, Shifty and Fu looked back at Movies sympathetically and hurried to catch up with Martin and Marcus who were looking in at the market.

The desolation there was almost complete. The wooden sheds were twisted and burnt black and soaked with hydrant-water. The entire place seemed as if it had been blasted by a hurricane of fire.

When Gerald, Shifty and Fu came up behind Marcus, they saw him pointing to a partly tattered and charred crocus bag of yams which had been roasted halfway through. The patches of food lay around the market yard in heaps of cinders, spiky and crumbling into ashes at the edges, and damp and sticky in other places.

The boys drew closer to the market railings and peered down into the wide expanse of the paved forecourt. They gazed at the chaotic mixture of destroyed wickerwork, straw and raffia products, fruits and vegetables, and the many items of haberdashery strewn around just where they had been dropped in panic or toppled when the rioters had launched their attack.

'I don't suppose the buses are running?' Martin asked.

'Shouldn't t'ink so, Missa Manson,' Marcus said, turning to look at an uprooted bus-stop near the entrance of the market gates.

'We'd better hurry, if we're walking down to Central, Dad,' Gerald said, slapping the saddle of his Rudge.

Martin nodded and walked away from the front of the market. He stopped when he got to the drug-store next door. That, too, had been burnt. The fire had not spread into the strong-room where the bottles of patent medicines and bulk chemicals were stored.

'That would've finished Cross Roads,' Martin said, waving his arms to take in the strong-room at the back of the store which he could see through a gaping hole in the left-hand show-glass.

'Would've finished off a few people, too,' Marcus said wryly.

Martin turned round slowly and faced the centre of Cross Roads. His face became suddenly haggard-looking and tense, and his eyes stared intently, while moving from one place to another over a fairly wide area in the bowl of the intersections. Gerald, Shifty and Fu, and Marcus, too, turned round and they began staring at the objects which Martin was looking at.

Spread out in front of them was a tangled mass of cracked stones, shattered half-bricks, splintered bottles and bruised and squashed sugar-cane stems.

After a while, Martin signalled with his right hand, which Marcus and the boys took to mean that it was time to move on. They did so, without commenting on the things they had been looking at, and without giving them a backward glance.

They headed down Slipe Road, and the after-effects were the same: broken windowpanes, shattered shop-frontages, jagged pieces of glass and wood and stone and mortar lying around all over the road.

West Race Course was the same. So was the top of East Street, where, added to the general mess, there were several overturned garbage-bins, tipped-over cars and vans and trucks, lopped-off tree branches and the ugly spectacle of two partly amputated giant hoardings swaying to and fro with their torn posters dangling and flapping eerily while a pack of starving mongrels divided their attention between rooting in a pile of fly-ridden garbage and yapping and jumping up to tear down the loose strips of the posters.

2

Martin's and Marcus's 'favourite' desk-sergeant was again on duty. He greeted the five callers with robust sarcasm; he smiled as soon as he saw them and asked, 'So you come to claim the body, eh?'

Martin ignored him and asked, 'Do you know when he's to be released?'

'Any time now,' he said off-handedly. 'You goin' to wait?'

'Yes.'

'Might be a long time, you know.'

'We'll wait. Thank you.'

'Good manners all of a sudden? Wha' 'appen? You gettin' wise to you'self an' t'ings roun' you at las'?'

Martin did not reply. He looked at Marcus and Gerald and led the way to the nearest long-bench.

The desk-sergeant grunted and started to arrange the duty book and the papers on his desk in preparation for his usual exhibition of play-acting, his customary exercise which came welling up out of the depths of his boredom and depression and years of futile small actions and even smaller thoughts.

Gerald, Shifty and Fu were watching him very closely. They had taken the end places on the long-bench. They were a matter of a few inches away from him. They had never been so near to a policeman before, and to a desk-sergeant at that. They looked at his large hands, and Gerald counted his fat fingers without knowing why he was doing so. Then, together with Shifty and Fu, he scrutinized the sergeant's face, dwelling on his bloodshot eyes, his bulbous nose, his pitted cheeks, his thick blue-black-pink speckled lips, and the coming spread of grey stubble on his chin.

Quite suddenly, Gerald told himself that he liked the man; there was something 'all right' about him; he was indeed 'as ugly as sin', but he looked like someone you'd meet outside in the street, not really like a 'big-time, high-powered' policeman who'd arrest you and 'throw away the key' or anything like that; he was funny, and nice too, in a sort of old-fashioned 'country come to town' way.

Gerald wondered why his father had been so abrupt with the sergeant, and also why Marcus had been so distant and cautious.

In a second, almost as though he had been reading Gerald's thoughts, the sergeant's voice boomed, 'Wha' school you goin' to, sonny boy?'

Gerald found himself standing at attention and saying, 'Kingston College, sir. All three of us.'

'You don't 'ave to stan' up for me, you know. Wha' you' name?'

'Gerald Manson, sir. That's my father.' Gerald pointed to Martin at the other end of the bench.

The sergeant pouted thoughtfully at the second half of the information, shook his head, and said, 'Nice young feller, you mus' stay out o' politics an' make a good, sensible livin' for you'self after you leave school.'

Gerald nodded, and then he sat down with correct humility,

with his head lowered slightly and his hands clasped. He wanted to show his respect for the sergeant; he liked him enormously.

'An' that goes for you two!' the sergeant boomed at Shifty and Fu.

Shifty and Fu bowed respectfully.

'Wha' you goin' to be when you grow up?' the sergeant asked.

'Not certain,' Shifty said.

'Neither me,' Fu said.

'Don't know yet,' Gerald stammered slowly, shyly.

'*Don't know?* Shame on you, young feller. Shame on all t'ree o' you.'

Martin and Marcus had overheard the conversation; indeed, they had been listening intently to every word, but they had not made the sergeant. aware of their interest; they kept looking towards the far corner of the room, with their backs half-turned.

'I suppose I'll make up my mind later on after Senior and Higher Schools,' Gerald said. 'That is, if I can pass them.'

'Same here,' Fu said.

'Me, too.' Shifty said.

'Exams is a good t'ing,' the sergeant said. 'I wish I'd passed some o' them when I was a boy, but I didn't 'ave you' sort o' chances.'

Gerald looked down at the floor and formed an inverted V with the points of his shoes. Shifty bowed his head and held the bridge of his nose between the thumb and first finger of his left hand. Fu grinned inanely, self-consciously.

The sergeant recognized the boys' embarrassment and said to them, 'We livin' t'rou' excitin' times, riot an' all that.'

Gerald looked up but not at the sergeant. He glanced at his father.

The sergeant's statement had caused Marcus to turn slightly; the sergeant noticed the shift in position and directed his next flow of words straight at him. He said, 'Plenty o' us feelin' our stren't' an' would like to show off wit' it an' cause commotion, but the law 'ave a long han' like a clothes-line.'

Martin got up and walked over to a half-open window at the far end of the room. Marcus followed him.

The sergeant smiled. Then he said, by way of changing the topic, 'Young Manson, wha' you' two frien's' name'?'

Gerald looked at Shifty and Fu.

Shifty said, 'Arnold Palmer, but the boys at school call me "Shifty Shanks".'

And Fu said, 'Leo Lockwood.' And he stopped short.

'An' the boys at school,' the sergeant said. 'Don't they call you by a special name?'

'Few of them do,' Fu said.

'Tell us then!' the sergeant boomed, and entreated good-humouredly.

Fu grinned sheepishly and said, 'Fu Manchu.'

The sergeant guffawed and tapped his forehead. Then he said, 'School-days. Good days, eh?' And he guffawed again.

Martin and Marcus turned and stared at him.

Gerald was convinced of his father's antipathy to the sergeant, and of Marcus's fear and loathing. He blamed it all on the rioting, on the unpleasant duties that the police had had to perform during the period, and on the fact that Crossman had been detained for so long. But he came back to the simple, unalterable opinion that he liked the sergeant. Then he tried to work out why he did. He teased his thoughts along and dredged up impressions and reasons that had to do with the sergeant's hopeless ugliness, his crude comedian's disarming personality, his fat untidiness, his chunky banana fingers, his mock-seriousness, and his obvious regard for education and respectability.

Gerald also wondered about the sergeant's early childhood, but he was not clear just what he was trying to conclude from his speculation.

In the meantime, the sergeant had gone back to his play-acting with his duty book and his papers.

Gerald suddenly remembered Big Man. He huddled close to Shifty and Fu and whispered, 'Do we tell about this morning?' He got no reaction, so he added, 'Do we tell our old people about Miller Street?'

Fu shook his head and pouted a silent 'No'.

Shifty shrugged non-committally.

It was left up to Gerald himself. He stared at his father, and back to the sergeant.

'What about you, Gerry?' Shifty whispered.

'It can wait,' Gerald said.

3

Alexander Crossman was released at about ten-thirty, a little over an hour after Martin, Marcus and the boys had got to the station.

He greeted Martin warmly and embraced him. He saluted Marcus and smiled at Gerald, Shifty and Fu, and he also patted Gerald's shoulder.

'The van's outside,' Martin told him.

'Where?'

'In the yard. It's been there since yesterday. Shall we check out?'

'Where to?'

'Up to my place. For breakfast and a chat about all that's happened since you've been inside.'

'O.K.'

Gerald looked at the two men and then he looked at the desk-sergeant and he knew instinctively that there was a great difference between what the sergeant seemed to be and what his father and Crossman were; the sergeant's dreams were essentially different from those of his father and Crossman.

Marcus offered to drive the van and Martin and Crossman piled in, while Gerald, Shifty and Fu mounted their Rudges; but as soon as they passed through the main gate of the station, they were stopped by Big Man, Horace and Preston who were waving excitedly and shouting Crossman's name with enormous pride and affection.

Marcus got out and opened the back of the van and they climbed in. On the way up East Street, Big Man explained emphatically, 'You see, Missa Crossman, this is wha' we been doin': we been waitin' outside Central from we 'ear say you goin' get release' today. We see when Marcus an' Missa Manson an' the youngsters go inside, so we decide to plan a little t'ing in you' 'onour like.'

'In *my* honour, Big Man?' Crossman asked. 'What?'

'Well, is like this,' Big Man said. 'We want you to drive straight to Race Course right now, an' you'll see wha' I mean.'

'We got a surprise for you a'right, sir,' Horace added.

'A right an' fittin' surprise, Missa Crossman,' Preston pressed the point further.

'O.K. by me,' Crossman said. 'We can stop at the Race Course on our way up to your place, Martin. What d'you think?'

'I'm not too sure,' Martin said thoughtfully, 'if you ought to be out in the street so soon, Alex. And the Race Course?'

'No 'arm can't come an' touch the Chief,' Preston urged.

'None at all,' Horace backed him up.

'We'll see to that,' Big Man said. 'Besides, you jus' got to go, Missa Crossman. You jus' got to.'

Crossman looked at Martin, and Martin winked.

'Race Course, Marcus,' Crossman said and rubbed his hands expectantly.

Marcus nodded, and hunched his shoulders over the steering-wheel.

CHAPTER NINE

1

Marcus drove furiously through the western entrance of the Race Course, and a mammoth crowd of well over five thousand people moved forward to meet the van. Crossman was extremely surprised but he understood the situation at a glance, and he knew exactly what he had to do.

He sprang out of the van and ran to the grandstand and leapt on to the dais a few feet away.

The crowd changed its direction and swarmed towards the foot of the dais on which Crossman was now standing with dignified composure. He waved his arms and clasped his fists in acknowledgement of the reception, and silence fell over the Race Course.

Martin, Marcus and Big Man struggled and fought their way to the side of the dais, mounted it in a leap and stood behind Crossman. Horace and Preston pressed through the tightly packed outer rim of the crowd and wedged themselves in front of Crossman's feet with their backs to the dais and their faces towards the waiting mass of the people.

Gerald, Shifty and Fu had parked their Rudges at a safe distance away and had climbed high into the tiers of seats in the grandstand behind Crossman.

The silence continued.

Martin, Marcus and Big Man glanced at one another, and then they smiled proudly in Crossman's direction.

Horace and Preston were standing with their feet apart, their arms folded and their chins arrogantly jutted at a sharp angle towards the passive faces before them.

Crossman made a quick, shrewd decision about what he was going to say and *how* he would say it. He was fully aware of what Marcus and Big Man expected of him. He took it for granted that

Horace and Preston, whom he did not know, certainly expected the same. On the other hand, he was also sure that what Martin expected to hear would be not precisely the same thing that the others wanted to hear, and definitely not in the same style. And yet, he was confident that he would be able to satisfy everybody.

'My people!' he called out.

The replies came pelting back at him with great warmth and affection and sincerity and respect: 'Yes, Chief!' 'Talk to we, Missa Crossman, sah!' 'We wit' you, Master!' The medley of responses soared in intensity and broke over the Race Course in a thunderclap of confused utterances.

Gerald and Shifty sat on the edge of their seat and waited. Fu clenched his fists.

Then Crossman held up his right hand, with the fingers pressed together and the edge of the palm turned towards the crowd, and he lowered it and raised it slowly two or three times in the manner of someone giving his blessing.

The emotion of the crowd subsided, and the responses died away.

Fu made a mental note of the way the people were dressed; they reminded him of the forlorn gathering in Big Man's yard. Their eyes were equally sad and piercing.

Silence.

'You see 'ow I come back to all o' you?' Crossman shouted.

'Yes, Chief, you come back to we!' 'You is we Saviour!' 'Talk to we, leader-man!' He had pushed them to the brink, and again, they responded with tremendous emotion.

He waved his arms for silence, and got it in a split second.

He looked to his left and saw Marcus smiling, and then he looked to his right and saw that Martin's face was expressionless.

He held out his arms and placed his wrists together and said, 'They arres' me but I walk out safe an' soun'.'

'Safe an' soun'!' the crowd chanted.

For no reason at all, Gerald suddenly recalled the desk-sergeant's face.

'An' now that I'm free again (t'anks to all o' you, because they wouldn't dare to touch a 'air on me head, wit' you to answer to), I goin' work 'ard for all o' you, my people.'

'Gawd bless you, Chief!' 'Good t'ing that, Missa Crossman!' 'We want you, Chief!'

'An' I goin' get a fair break for you an' for all you' pickney.'

'That's right, Chief!' 'Wit' you, Master!'

'I tell you, my people, we goin' walk wit' we 'ead up in the air like proud people from now on.'

'Show the way, Chief!' a man bellowed from the front line.

Gerald was still thinking of the desk-sergeant, when Shifty nudged him. He pointed to the man who had just shouted up to Crossman. Gerald nodded and said, 'Yes, I agree. Just like the man who showed us Big Man's yard.' Shifty nodded.

'Right,' Crossman said rather conversationally. 'Quite right that. *I* can show you an' all o' my people the way to prosperity an' 'appiness if you join up like one man an' put you' trus' an' confidence in me, I can show you the way to beat the Devil. But before I can do that, you will 'ave to give me the proper sort o' support wit' you' numbers. An' that mean that you got to join the Union firs' t'ing on Monday mawnin'. All o' you mus' join, workin' man or no. You mus' come an' see me at the cabinet shop an' sign up. An' remember, if you make the Union work, it will work for you.'

Horace and Preston shouted, 'If you make it work, it will work for you!'

And the crowd responded, 'True word!'

Just after that, a cry of 'Babylon break!' rang out from the outer rim of the gathering. It was followed by 'Watch out, Chief, they come back for you!'

Crossman looked right round the Race Course and saw a vast cordon of policemen approaching the crowd slowly. They were walking about three yards apart from one another and precisely in step. Each policeman had his baton drawn.

Gerald, Shifty and Fu stood and began counting the policemen.

Crossman turned to his right and saw the same inspector who had taken him in the day before coming towards the grandstand.

'Wind it up, Alex,' Martin whispered. His voice was charged with authority.

Crossman gazed at him as if he had not heard him. Then he

switched his gaze to the inspector who was now mounting the dais.

'Go on, Alex,' Martin said. 'Mention Monday morning again, and tell them to go away quietly. Begin *now*.'

Crossman cleared his throat. He was grateful for Martin's advice. He spread his arms wide and said, 'My people, please listen to me.' He paused. The inspector smiled. Crossman bowed to him and turned back to the crowd. 'Peace an' love, my people! That is the message from me an' from the inspector standin' 'ere beside me.'

There was no response from the crowd.

The inspector moved closer to Crossman.

Crossman continued, 'An' remember that the state o' emergency is still goin' on, so we've got to obey the law.'

The inspector smiled again and slapped his trouser-leg with his stick.

Crossman invited him to share the central spot on the dais, but the inspector waved the invitation graciously away and remained where he was standing.

Gerald stared down at his father, but he could not see his face. Shifty looked at the railing on which the Rudges had been parked. He quickly gauged the distance from the grandstand, and relaxed. Fu was watching the inspector closely.

'My people,' Crossman said, embracing the crowd with open arms, 'the inspector didn't want to join me because he's got confidence in me an' because he trusts me as you' leader. You mus' give me you' trust too. An' remember Monday mawnin'.'

'Monday mawnin'!' the crowd roared.

Crossman held back until there was a lull in the commotion, and then he said, 'I will be waitin' to sign you up, to serve you, to fight for you, to protec' you, even if I 'ave to *die* for you!'

The crowd went wild.

The inspector moved towards Crossman.

Martin, Marcus and Big Man moved in on the inspector.

But Crossman spread his arms again and the crowd suddenly stifled its emotional fervour.

The inspector froze.

Martin, Marcus and Big Man inched backwards to their original positions.

Crossman smiled broadly, held up his right hand, 'blessed' the crowd, using the graceful gesture of his pressed fingers, and said, 'An' now, let us go 'ome an' res' on the Lord's day o' prayer an' contemplation. We will meet again tomorrow at the cabinet shop.' He paused. Then he walked down to the front of the dais.

The crowd was dead still.

Gerald, Shifty and Fu were poised to leap off the grandstand.

Crossman clenched his fists and waved them in a circular fashion over his head. 'Peace!' he called out. 'Peace an' love!'

The cordon of police had tightened round the crowd.

Martin stepped between the inspector and Crossman and placed his hand on Crossman's shoulder. Big Man and Marcus came up to him and waited for Martin to make the first move.

The inspector backed away and made room for Crossman to pass him by. But Crossman bowed, changed direction and walked to the edge of the dais.

Horace and Preston rushed to the spot where they reckoned Crossman was about to jump. They held out their hands to take his weight. He grasped their wrists and slid down easily. His landing was dignified.

In the meantime, Marcus had backed the van up towards Crossman. Martin, Big Man, Horace and Preston got in. Crossman leant against the open door, turned to the dispersing crowd and waved. Then he slipped in beside Marcus and slammed the door.

The van drove out of the Race Course to the resounding cheers of 'Monday mawnin', Chief!' 'Union for we!' And as soon as the van got out to West Race Course, the tumultuous singing began:

'We – will fol–low Miss–a Cross–man
We – will fol–low Miss–a Cross–man
We – will fol–low Miss–a Cross–man
We – will fol–low Miss–a Cross–man
'til – we – die!'

2

Sitting well back from the sparkling chromium handles of their Rudges, with their hands resting stylishly akimbo, Gerald, Shifty and Fu cruised left round Club Rostov, away from West Race Course, turned right at Torrington Bridge, into Slipe Road, and headed towards Cross Roads.

Feeling elated and self-importantly privileged at what they had just witnessed in the Race Course, they recalled Crossman's statement about the Union, discussed it among themselves, and afterwards began to wonder silently what it would be like and what it would really do.

When they got to Cross Roads, Shifty pointed in the direction of the broad concrete steps in front of the post office and said, 'There he goes again, believe it or not!'

Gerald and Fu looked to their right and saw a man bending over a bundle of sugar-cane stems and trying to tie it with a length of sash-cord. The bundle was very large and the sash-cord was not long enough. The man's head and arms were bandaged, and he had a plaster-cast on his left leg.

'Good old Bag-'n'-Pan!' Gerald saluted him with lively familiarity.

'You can't stop him no how,' Fu said.

As they passed by, they called out his name affectionately and waved to him.

Bag-'n'-Pan looked up, blinked, touched his bandaged head, recognized them with extreme difficulty and waved back.

Gerald, feeling a compulsive urge and unable to resist it, corkscrewed the upper part of his body to face Bag-'n'-Pan and shouted, 'Big day Monday morning coming, Bag-'n'-Pan! Union day!'

Bag-'n'-Pan smiled, shrugged unconcernedly and bent intently once more over his bundle of sugar-cane stems.

GLOSSARY

ADVENTITIOUS ROOTS: Bulky, gnarled loops of roots growing above the ground and spreading outwards from the base of certain very large tropical shade-trees, especially the banyan.

BANDANAS: Large colourful handkerchief-cloths, used as head-wraps by some Kingston market vendors, and by many women in the rural areas of Jamaica.

BANYAN: Giant fig-tree, with adventitious roots, imported into the West Indies from India.

BERBICE CHAIRS: Spacious wooden veranda chairs, originally popular in Berbice, Guyana.

BOWL-FOR-BAT: A single wicket game of cricket, with one batsman and any number of self-appointed bowlers and fieldsmen, each bowling and fielding independently for the batsman's position at the wicket.

'COOLIE FOOT' SUGAR: Dark brown crude 'wet' sugar. According to folk myth, it was said to be trampled on by Indian sugar plantation workers.

DUPPY: A ghost. Often spoken about with trepid affection. Usually mentioned in the retelling of old plantation stories and folk-tales, told late at night in the country districts.

ESPALIER: A wooden or wire lattice framework on which vines and shrubs are trained.

THE GLEANER: The Daily Gleaner is Jamaica's leading newspaper.

JIPPA JAPPA HATS: Men's white straw hats, with a narrow black band, originally imported into Jamaica from Japan, and subsequently manufactured by straw-craftsmen in Kingston.

JOSEPH'S-COAT: Low-growing decorative shrub, with fairly large variegated leaves.

'PAN HEAD': A special constable in plain clothes, usually patrolling on a bicycle, and particularly feared by schoolboy would-be offenders.

PEPPERPOT SOUP: There are many types of pepperpot throughout the West Indies. The Jamaican dish is a highly seasoned meat-and-vegetable stew, flavoured with hot peppers.

PICKNEY: An affectionate Jamaican Creole expression for a young child.

PWD: Public Works Department.

RAM-GOAT ROSES: Sometimes called 'Periwinkle'. The blooms are white or light purple or yellow, and the growths are low to the ground and modestly fragrant.

RUDGE WHITWORTH: A favourite make of British bicycle among Jamaican secondary school scholarship winners during the early post-war years.

SISAL: Fibre prepared from leaves of the Agave plant, used for making cordage, rope and doormats.

SLIPE ROAD/SLIPEN ROAD: These are distinctly different roads (in what used to be called Lower Saint Andrew and is now Kingston), which run, more or less, parallel to each other.

WESTERN ROLL: An American style of high-jumping, replacing the traditional scissor-action leap. The 'Western' is a face-downwards half-roll over the crossbar.

WORD-MERCHANT: A lover of words for the sake of words. A speaker with the capacity for exhibiting his showy vocabulary.

ABOUT THE AUTHOR

Andrew Salkey was born in Panama in 1928 of Jamaican parents, and brought up in Jamaica. A major figure in Caribbean literature, he published five novels; two collections of short stories; four collections of poetry; eight novels for children; two important travel books; and numerous groundbreaking anthologies of Caribbean writing in the 1960s and 1970s. In London from the 1950s through to the '70s, he worked as a broadcaster for the BBC *Caribbean Voices* programme and was later deeply involved in the Caribbean Artists Movement. In 1976 he relocated to Hampshire College in Amherst, in the United States, where he died in 1995.

Other titles in this celebrated quartet of books for children...

Andrew Salkey, *Hurricane*
ISBN: 9781845231804; pp. 102; May 2011 [1964]; £6.99

Hurricane is the gripping story of a natural disaster and the 13-year-old Kingston boy who lives to tell the tale. While the wind turns trees to splinters, darkness swallows the land and rains lash the roof, all Joe and his family can do is worry, and wait, and hope. The first in Salkey's quartet of illustrated children's novels about Jamaica's natural and manmade cataclysms, *Hurricane* won the 1967 German Children's Book Prize.

Andrew Salkey, *Earthquake*
ISBN: 9781845231828; pp. 104; May 2011 [1965]; £6.99

Siblings Ricky, Doug and Polly spend summer with their grandparents in the Jamaican countryside. While playing games of 'Three on a Desert Island' on a sunbaking day in July, the children feel the earth itself move beneath their feet. Is it part of their vivid imaginations – or is it the sign of a coming earthquake? *Earthquake* is a lively, illustrated masterpiece.

Andrew Salkey, *Drought*
ISBN: 9781845231835; pp. 122; May 2011 [1966]; £6.99

It is dry season. The small village of Nain is suffering. Its people, livestock and crops have all been affected and things are looking bleak. But Seth Stone and friends Man Boy, Benjie, Double Ugly and Mango Head are determined to take matters into their own hands – with unexpected results. A lavishly illustrated story of hardship and resilience.